I0613478

The Edge of Night

By

Jeffery Martin Botzenhart

ALL RIGHTS RESERVED

No part of this book may be reproduced or transmitted in any form or by any means, electronic or mechanical, including photocopying, recording, or by any information storage and retrieval system, without permission in writing from the author, except in the case of brief quotations embodied in reviews.

Publisher's Note:

This is a work of fiction. All names, characters, places, and events are the work of the author's imagination.

Any resemblance to real persons, places, or events is coincidental.

Solstice Publishing - www.solsticepublishing.com

Copyright 2019 – Jeffery Martin Botzenhart

Chapter One

"Why doesn't it get dark?" Sage asked his mom, softly, as she tucked him in bed.

Nora's voice held a smooth gentle tone.

"Well, we live in the sunlight. Our skyjammer is solar powered. Without the sun's rays, and solar winds, we would fall out of the sky. I'm sure I've told you this before."

"Why is Dad scared of the dark? What's in the dark that's not in the light?" Sage continued, hugging his pillow. This was something they hadn't spoken of.

"There are *people* who live in the dark who we don't really understand and who don't understand us," she explained, sitting down on the edge of the bed.

"Do they want to hurt us?"

"No, sweetheart," she said, tenderly running her hands through his hair. "We're just so very different from them."

"How?"

"My goodness, so many questions," she commented. Being highly persistent for a ten year old boy, Nora understood, by the way Sage looked at her, that his question would require an answer. "After the war, when people had to abandon the Earth's surface, some could only leave during the day with others only being able to leave after dark."

"Why?"

Knowing a day would come when Sage needed to be told about the Earth's tragic history, Nora wasn't sure if she was prepared enough to reveal all she knew. The emotional wounds from their departure still felt raw and painful and would expose the heartbreak she continued suffering even after all these years. Nora silently wondered if she would ever be ready to tell him all that happened. Could she once more confront the ghosts she hid from? Exhaling and smiling, Nora chose not to answer his question.

"Good night, sweetheart."

"Good night, Mom," Sage said, snuggling deeper against his pillow. Leaning down, she kissed him on his cheek before pulling down his window shade and closing his door behind her as she left.

***

As always, the sun shone brightly overhead as Caleb commanded the helm of their skyjammer. The shimmering, solar sails capturing the wind were gathering energy enabling them to maintain a constant, cruising speed keeping them in the sunlight. There was clear sailing through the sky for miles ahead as they passed over large, dark clouds shielding the Earth below.

"So how many questions were there tonight?" Caleb asked.

"Several, with many more I think." Nora held his hand while leaning her head against his shoulder.

"Someday we'll tell him everything he needs to know. But, for now, I think we should enjoy what innocence he has left before reality changes his world," Caleb suggested, as he leaned his head against hers. Seeing Nora close her eyes, he leaned into her ear. "You should get some sleep. You look tired."

"In a little while. I'm enjoying your company." Turning her head, she kissed him on his cheek, causing him to smile. "You need a shave." She kissed him once more.

"*What*? Doesn't five-o'clock shadow make a guy look handsome?"

"Devastatingly handsome," Nora answered, while caressing his cheek. "On second thought, you should keep it."

With her resting her head, again, against his shoulder, Caleb was happy for the company. Yet, a thought he couldn't get rid of bothered him to the point of looking at her.

"Do you ever think about what it's like down there now?" he asked.

"Sometimes. I remember, when we left, my father tried to make it all sound like a big adventure. I'm not sure my mother felt the same way. What about you?"

"Most of the time I try not to think about it…but sometimes I can't help it."

"Do you wonder where they are? Your brothers?"

"Yeah." Thinking back to crowd on board one of the last skyjammers lifting off from the Arizona desert before a massive dust storm hit. The pain of those final minutes still hurt as much as it did all those years ago. Hearing his dad say that their skyjammer was too heavy by a few hundred pounds, he recalled his older brothers, Luke and Wyatt, helping unload some unnecessary supplies to lighten the load. He later found out his dad was lying. After luring them off the skyjammer, his dad took off, leaving Luke and Wyatt behind. Learning that his dad, who had served in the military, suffered from paranoid episodes as part of his post-traumatic stress disorder, at the time when they left he was delusional, believing his older sons were enemy soldiers. A month later, after he drunkenly confessed this, Caleb remembered his dad shooting himself in the head, leaving Caleb, only sixteen, alone and afraid.

Glancing back, his eyes searched the horizon behind them for any traces of the edge of night. Having been warned by his dad about the dangerous people existing there, he was always weary of any traces of darkness in the sky. Although he and Nora never spoke of this, Caleb knew she held the same fears as his.

The old radar system onboard issued an alarm, pulling Caleb from this nightmarish memory. Moving away from Nora, he spied through a telescope near the helm.

"We're heading toward another skyjammer," he revealed.

"Can you see anyone?" Nora sounded hopeful in asking. It had been almost a year since they last saw another skyjammer having living people on board. But suspicious of their intentions, as piracy was not uncommon, they kept their distance communicating only by short wave radio. Unconvinced, they held no hostile intentions, Caleb steered them away from these survivors, believing they were better off alone than with them.

"I don't see anyone," Caleb answered. "The solar panels seem intact otherwise it would have fallen from the sky. But its speed is too slow to keep going much longer. There's a huge hole in the fuselage and it looks like there was a fire." He paused for a moment. "Maybe we can salvage something from it."

"Do you think…their bodies are still on board?" Nora wondered, clearly hesitant in asking. Having salvaged parts and supplies from a few other derelict skyjammers, Caleb understood her concern. Once before, while scavenging on a skyjammer similar to the one they were approaching, Caleb had found the bodies of an entire family. Finding no food or water, he guessed they may have starved to death. All skyjammers are equipped with greenhouses and water vapor, collecting devices. On this particular one, the greenhouse was barren of plants and the water vapor device had been taken apart as if someone had tried to repair it.

"I don't know," he answered. "But…we should still try to see what we can salvage."

Retracting the solar sails to slow the skyjammer, Caleb maneuvered their skyjammer as near as he could over top of the other one, making sure his solar sails remained clear of touching the other skyjammer.

"Hold our position," he instructed Nora. "I'm gonna send a ladder down through our bottom hatch to its top hatch." Kissing her before leaving, he grinned. "I won't be long. I promise."

Deafening sounds of the rushing wind robbed Caleb of his hearing after opening the bottom hatch. Dropping a rope ladder, weighed down by large magnets on its end, the ladder secured the skyjammer when touching its metal fuselage. Tying a safety rope to his belt, Caleb began climbing down holding tight to the ladder while being assaulted by heated gusts of air.

Once he reached the top of the derelict skyjammer, Caleb forced the top hatch open and climbed down inside. His eyes were instantly drawn to the burn marks across the helm. Studying the damage, he knew right away that the cause had nothing to do with internal malfunctions. The helm had been riddled by bullets, no doubt creating sparks melting the wiring.

Finding nothing salvageable here, he moved on, climbing down a set of steps to the main living quarters. Everything of value had either been destroyed or stolen. All evidence suggested that pirates had ransacked this skyjammer, leaving him with one question. *Where were the passengers?* Passing unmade beds in the bunk quarters, and seeing a smashed mirror in the bathroom, he wandered further to the greenhouse. Not surprisingly, the fruits and vegetables once grown here had been harvested and the overhead windows shattered.

He found the last door leading into the engine room housing batteries and devices keeping the skyjammer soaring above the Earth's surface. Caleb stepped inside slowly. Glancing at the water tank, he noticed a gaping hole in the side believing all the water it held had been taken with what remained, having evaporated from the heat. Broken glass and metal debris littered the floor he walked across while surveying the damage.

Caleb finally came across something worth salvaging. Seemingly untouched, when reaching for one of the reserve solar batteries, he failed to notice a trap left by the pirates. When touching the battery, to detach wires leading to the solar panels, an electrical charge surged through his body, scorching his fingers and robbing him of his breath. Feeling his pulse racing and throbbing pain in his chest, Caleb stumbled back, colliding with the wall.

Smelling pungent fumes, Caleb began coughing when seeing smoke seeping through from a vent on the floor. Recognizing the stench as ammonia, he knew only a few moments were left before the gas would be ignited causing an explosion that would not only destroy this skyjammer, but his own as well.

Staggering away, his vision growing blurred with his lungs burning and his chest tight with pain, Caleb managed to climb back up to the helm and over to the top hatch. Believing he would be dead within minutes and not wanting Nora and Sage to suffer in seeing him die, Caleb struggled in managing to detach the ladder from the fuselage, sending it flinging away. Staggering back to the helm, robbed of his final breaths by the pain he suffered in his chest, Caleb steered the skyjammer away, with it spiraling out of control. Clutching his chest when gasping for air, he watched the dark clouds covering the Earth coming closer and closer until all immersed within blackness.

***

A hush fell over the students as Professor Valorian entered the classroom. The impression of authority for which he exuded proved always beyond question. He stood confidently, as an imposing figure, with his towering height and shapely bald head. His expectations for his pupils were simple. Perfection, nothing less would be tolerated. He knew immediately if a student would excel or fail in his class. Those who would excel held fear in their eyes.

And then there was Marisol. Her expression exuded a casual calmness which, from anyone else, would have vexed him to no end. Her insatiable thirst for knowledge truly set her apart from all other twelve year old students. She was his diamond in a sea of glass and she knew this to be true. By the asking of a simple question Marisol could manipulate the classroom lecture to satisfy her curiosity on topics not planned for discussion. Valorian chided himself for being drawn away from the task at hand yet reveled in her ability to subtly challenge the authority he commanded. Ultimately, in his eyes she was not merely his favorite student. She was his *only* student.

"Good morning class," he greeted, projecting his usual deep tone of authority. "Today we shall review that which we have learned, and will be evaluated on, for our next session's mid-term examinations. Who will be bold enough to start?" Professor Valorian already knew the answer to this question. He had thrown down the gauntlet and she leapt with ravenous intensity. "Marisol, please begin."

Although her voice spoke with a soft lilt to it, Marisol's tone held a great authority of its own.

"In the year 2117, civil unrest broke out among the lunar colonists due in large part to territorial and natural resource disputes. The unrest spread rapidly to the governments on Earth who were already preoccupied with a cyber-conflict among the industrialized nations. Within weeks, this conflict spread to conventional warfare and eventually led to the use of weapons of mass destruction. Arguably, at best, it is assumed that roughly seventy-five percent of the world population perished in this conflict. It is also assumed that the lunar colonists perished due to a lack of available supplies being sent to them. All communications have ceased between Earth and the Moon. With major population centers on Earth decimated, and economies and infrastructure destroyed beyond repair, neither side would concede defeat. Biological and chemical weapons were then unleashed upon the remaining population as both accused the other of genocide."

Professor Valorian interrupted Marisol, briefly.

"Brilliant as usual," he complimented her. "Please enlighten the class as to the ramifications of the use of these biological and chemical agents."

Marisol nodded her head.

"For many the biological weapons caused paralysis and eventually death," she continued. "For others, there were virtually no effects. And, for the remaining few, their genetics were immediately and irrevocably altered. For these individuals, albino-like traits caused their flesh to be instantly scorched when in direct contact with sunlight resulting in a most, painful death. They were forced indoors and underground to live in the darkness."

Marisol cast a casual glance at her classmates, all of whom had pale, white skin and white hair. Each of them had this genetic alteration, as did Marisol herself. She, however, was also different from the others being of African-American descent. The coloration of her skin held a darker, and somewhat exotic, tone. In direct contrast, Professor Valorian's pale, white complexion appeared luminous.

With a bow of his head, Professor Valorian encouraged Marisol to finish.

"The Earth had been altered to a toxic wasteland. No longer inhabitable by those still alive, an exodus of the remaining population left Earth to its lonesome, tragic end. It is unfortunate that not all found escape. It is assumed that those forced to remain succumbed to disease and famine.

No contact has, to this point, been made with those on the Earth's surface.

Two populations found exile in the sky. Limited, technological advances were embraced by those who selected solar power. These people, known to us as *daylighters,* live in vessels referred to as skyjammers. A skyjammer is a solar-powered airship that traditionally consists of a helm, a kitchen and bath, one or two small bedrooms, and a greenhouse for growing fruits and vegetables. Mechanical systems which employ the use of steam energy generated by solar waves are the secondary sources of power. Wind turbines are also utilized. In addition, they employ more primitive technology such as short-wave radios. These people tend to be vegetarian in nature due to the lack of available meat. From the gathered research done on them, it is believed they are nomadic in nature and scavenge what they find from salvaging parts and supplies from abandoned skyjammers. Rumors persist of skyports and a grand armada of these skyjammers...yet this has never yielded solid confirmation for either."

An uncharacteristic smile crossed over Professor Valorian's face.

"And what of those who could only dwell within the darkness?" he questioned Marisol.

"They travel through dark sunless skies on nuclear-powered orbiting cities. Here we are," Marisol said, as she displayed a sly smile.

Chapter Two

Nine years later

"Tell me a story," Sage begged, as he lay his head down on his pillow.

"I thought you were too old for stories?" Nora questioned her now nineteen year old son. To her he offered his usual smile, one which reflected images of his dad. Never had she found the ability to deny him anything when he smiled at her this way, feeling closer to Caleb each time when Sage reminded her of him. After all these years, the ache of being without him had lost none of its intensity. In truth, she missed Caleb more and more with each passing day.

"What story would you like to hear?"

"Tell me how you and dad met. You've never told me this before."

Sage was right. This was a story Nora had never spoken of. For a moment, she sat on the edge of his bed as she prepared herself for the torture she was about to unleash upon herself.

"Well…it was twenty-one years ago. My family, my mother and father and younger sister and I, was traveling through the sky with a group of skyjammers that had banded together. Our group was one of the last to leave what remained of Boston before a chemical storm destroyed what was left of the city. It was my father's hope that we would eventually find the armada and stay with them."

Nora stayed quiet for a moment as she had come to the part of the story where she met Caleb. Sage sat up, taking hold of her hands which were fidgeting in her lap.

"You don't have to tell me this story. I'm sorry. I don't want to make you sad." Nora looked into his eyes and saw her reflection and Caleb's as well.

"No, I want to tell this story. I want you to know everything," she responded. "Your dad was what people on Earth referred to as a drifter. He was on his own with no family to speak of. Your dad's mother had died when Nebraska was first bombed in the early part of the war. His father was delusional and mentally unstable due to post-traumatic stress disorder suffered when he was a soldier. After leaving your dad's brothers in the desert, eventually your grandfather killed himself, leaving your dad alone aboard their skyjammer. He was only sixteen at the time.

"Anyway, when your dad joined our group at one of the sky ports that no longer exist, my father was extremely wary of him. He wanted to drive him off but the others in our group liked him very much. What was not to like? Caleb was a handsome, carefree young man. Extremely polite and wise beyond his years he was. I fell deeply in love with him from the first moment when we met. This gave my father even more reasons to want him gone.

"We spent a lot of time together within the two weeks he stayed with the group. I would always make up some excuse to see him. After the second week of being with us, Caleb told the members of our group his plans to leave. He had heard some rumors that the armada was flying north of the equator, somewhere near what once was Cuba.

"I went to see him the night before he left. We talked for the longest time about life before the war and life as it turned out to be. Having been born in Greenville, Nebraska, he missed the wide open spaces where he played with his brothers when he was a boy. And he talked about life in the refugee camps in Arizona, how crowded they were…as well as the violence. He wanted to find the armada, but not stay. He just wanted to know it existed."

"Why wouldn't he have stayed with the armada?"

"Like I said, he was a drifter. But more than that, I believe he was afraid. I think the time he spent in the refugee camp left him with some haunting memories. He never told me details about being there but, I knew from what I was told by others, how terrible those places were."

"So how did you end up leaving with him?"

"I asked him if I could go with him and he said yes, but only with my father's blessing. You see, your dad had also fallen in love with me. That was one of the happiest moments of my life. We went to speak to my father about this. Naturally, he refused to let me go with Caleb. I was bitter about this which led to my father and I having a terrible argument. I told him I would never speak to him again. I kept my promise."

"How did you keep that promise?" Sage interrupted, quietly.

"Once Caleb left he discovered a stowaway aboard his skyjammer, me. He wanted to turn back and return me to my family. I was able to change his mind, though. It only took three words from me to convince Caleb to let me stay with him."

"What were those three words?" Sage asked, before yawning deeply as his eyes grew heavy.

"I love you," Nora replied. After a moment of silence, Nora looked over to her son. Sage had fallen into a deep sleep. His arms were stretched up with his hands at rest under his head, just how Caleb used to sleep. Sage was so very much like his father. He had his father's handsome features, especially his beautiful brown eyes. He also possessed his father's intelligence and knowledge of how things worked. Sage had mastered everything from how to run and repair the solar panels, wind turbines, and the water vapor, collection device. Over time, he also learned how to salvage parts and scavenge when encountering abandoned skyjammers. His first time doing this, when he was just sixteen, was her most frightening experience since losing Caleb. Although nothing went wrong, just watching him was like reliving her worst nightmare.

Nora never revealed to Sage the truth of how Caleb died. The story she told him, only once, was of how he became sick and passed away suddenly. After that, he never asked to hear this story again, for which she was glad. But, whenever lying down to sleep, this was the first thing running through her mind every time.

One other lesson she made certain to teach Sage was of the dangers of pirates. Although, through these past nine years they hadn't encountered any, Nora believed they were lucky. In her heart, she knew that out there somewhere they were waiting. Having no weapons aboard to defend against pirates, Nora made sure both she and Sage stayed vigilant in watching for signs of them.

Leaving Sage, Nora returned to the helm and stared blankly out toward the horizon. Having told Sage the story of how she and Caleb met, her thoughts were now consumed in missing him. Wondering if she would be greeted by him someday when she died, this notion both comforted and frightened her. Although desperate to be with Caleb again, knowing that Sage would be left alone, broke her heart. He was the only reason keeping her alive. They had never spoken about what would happen after she was gone. Sage always seemed worried about her as if he understood that, someday, he would find himself alone. Maybe this was a conversation they needed to have. Like pirates, death loomed somewhere beyond the horizon, waiting for a terrible moment to appear.

Turning on the short-wave radio, deafening static blared until she adjusted the volume. Almost two years ago she heard a faint, almost unintelligible voice, sounding through the speaker. But, since then, nothing had been heard. Every day, though, she turned the radio on hoping to catch voices communicating and possibly leading them to the armada she still believed was out there.

Aside from basic survival, Nora knew that finding others would be essential for Sage's future. Even if they never found the armada, if at least they could find someone kind to travel with, then Sage wouldn't be alone.

Jarred alert from her thoughts, by unexpected turbulence, Nora stared ahead at fluid waves of heat flowing like sheer curtains. Violent flashes of lightning preceded echoing thunder from the fast approaching solar storm. Fearing the sails would be wrenched from the skyjammer's fuselage, Nora frantically attempted to retract them. Screaming out when a lightning bolt struck the helm, she shielded her face with her hands from an explosion of sparks caused by a power surge.

Falling to her knees, and rolling from side to side, Nora's body thrust back against the wall when the skyjammer was captured by the scorching winds of a solar vortex, sending it spinning through the sky. Over the roar of the storm, she thought she heard the wind turbines and solar sails being ripped away. Gripping the helm, she pulled herself up in time to see a fiery, red sky and web-like bolts of lightning. Holding on to the helm with what strength she had left, when one of her hands lost grip, Nora knew she couldn't hold on much longer. Glancing toward the blistering horizon, after taking one last breath, her fingers slipped and she let go.

***

Suffering pain from what seemed to be throbbing from every part of his body, Sage took shallow breaths of scorching air while blinking his eyes open. A burning, stinging sensation over his right eyes left him thinking he might have been cut there. Confused and lightheaded, at first, everything he saw seemed clouded and out of focus. Blinding pain radiating from the back of his head felt like it pierced his skull, causing him to clench his eyes closed. Once this subsided, he again opened his eyes, this time seeing much clearer. Yet, there, in front of him appeared well beyond anything he could imagine.

"I bid you greetings from the living," a young man similar in age to him offered through an English accent. Tall and lanky, the man, dressed in a black tuxedo jacket with matching pants and a grey vest over a red shirt, took off his top hat and slightly bowed to him. "I believe introductions are in order as dictated by the ceremony of such occasion." He placed his hand to his chest. "My esteemed host, I....am Lord Amphetamine." He motioned to the side with his hand. "This sublime creature is Lady Heroin." Glancing to his left, Sage noticed a young woman bow to him. Pale in complexion and having blonde shoulder-length hair, the tattered, ivory-colored, lace dress she wore reminded him of vintage fashions worn by women from photographs taken from the early twentieth century. Adorning her head was a brimmed hat and hung around her neck linked to chains were gears and antique keys.

Drawn away from looking at her, Sage was presented with final introductions.

"And these two strapping masses are Sir Adrenaline and Sir Lithium, both knights of the sun realm." Seeing two tall, muscular men flanking the first man, Sage swallowed hard, worried they might hurt him. "My friend, no harm will come to you. On my honor, you have my word," Lord Amphetamine assured him, apparently understanding the fear in his eyes.

Looking around at his familiar surroundings, everything in sight was either damaged or upended. Wondering if they had ransacked the skyjammer, Sage realized people he'd only heard stories of had become reality. There before him stood the pirates.

"Please don't hurt me and my mom. Take whatever you want," he begged.

"What we are in dire need of is your skyjammer," Lord Amphetamine responded, passing strange glances between them. "The solar storm irrevocably damaged our own, the *glorious Psychotropic*. With no other choice, we were forced to scuttle her and commandeer what is left of yours."

"Again, no harm will come to you. You are safe," Lady Heroin offered, noticing his distress, when kneeling before him.

"Where is my mom? What have you done with her?" Sage blurted out, his senses fully returned. Then, realizing both his hands and legs were tied to the chair, he was sitting on, Sage struggled to get lose.

"I beg your forgiveness," Lord Amphetamine said. "Uncertainty of your reaction to our presence led to the need for restraining you. As for your mother, my friend, I regret to say that we found no one else here aboard your skyjammer. Believe me, all was thoroughly searched."

"But…where is she?" Sage uttered, his eyes large and his heart wedged in his throat.

"There is…significant damage to the helm. The windows have been blown out. It is possible she…may have…fallen, or was possibly pulled out, when the helm depressurized."

Swallowing hard, his heart broke in reeling with finding out that his mom was gone. Unable to hold back his tears, they streamed down his face, soaking his cheeks with his head hanging low.

"Indeed, you have our deepest sympathy for your tragic loss, my friend," Lord Amphetamine added.

Cautiously moving close to him, Lady Heroin caressed his cheek, wiping away his tears. Easing then onto his lap, she pulled Sage's face to shoulder and held him close.

"In time, the sorrow shall pass and peace will exist in its stead. You will see," she whispered, running her hand across his bare shoulder in comfort.

Before Sage could say anything, Sir Adrenaline pointed out after looking through a telescope.

"The white city approaches, my Lord."

Seeing the apprehension on his expression, Sage was surprised when Lord Amphetamine commanded, "Unbound his hands and legs." Then looking directly at Sage, he said, "My sincere regret for this, my friend. I am forced to amend my earlier words. For now, you are a means to an end. Trust though, for we shall see each other once more." Feeling a harsh blow against the back of his head, Sage slumped down to the floor as everything grew blurry and then dark.

Chapter Three

The alarm from her visual, communication panel awakened Marisol, abruptly, from a restful sleep. Before climbing in bed, she'd spent several hours trying to fix an old radio she had found a week ago in some captured wreckage from an old skyjammer. She had spoken into the radio but no one answered. Rubbing the sleep from her eyes before accepting the message, she noticed it having been sent with high importance.

Marisol instantly recognized the face of her former professor from ten years prior. Valorian had ascended to the highest, official position of their floating metropolis, New London. During her school years, she was constantly by his side, either aiding him with his research or debating theories. After graduation, Marisol was offered a position within the Cultural Ministry, her field of specialty being the study of daylighter artifacts.

"Governor Valorian, what an honor to speak to you once more," Marisol offered, with great respect.

"My dear, Marisol, I profusely apologize for such a late contact. A matter of great urgency has come to my attention, one that directly should involve you. New London has encountered the debris of a skyjammer. Unexpectedly, we have captured a very…much…alive…daylighter. How soon should we expect your arrival at the Cultural Ministry?" His question went unanswered. Marisol had rapidly left upon hearing the word 'daylighter.'

***

Valorian appeared highly impressed as to how quickly she arrived by train to the ministry. When seeing him standing there her questions rapidly burst forth.

"Where is the daylighter? Is it a man, woman, or child? What language does it speak? Old or young? Any noticeable injuries?"

Amused by her insatiable curiosity, Valorian calmed her by holding his hand up to silence her questions.

"A young man, somewhat younger than you perhaps, was found unconscious within the wreckage of the skyjammer. Medical technicians were able to awaken him but the young man proved highly distressed by his surroundings and has armed himself with a surgical blade. He is safely trapped within an examination room. He requires medical attention but is extremely frightened when any of the staff attempt to go near him. I was hoping you might enter the room and persuade him to lower the blade so that his injuries can be tended to. In no way do I wish to place your life in jeopardy. However, a woman's touch may be just what we need, especially a woman trained in martial arts…and whom is quite capable of defending herself."

Valorian led Marisol to an observation window for the examination room. Only they could see inside; the daylighter could not see them. Marisol moved close to the glass and looked into the room. Partially concealed in the corner was the young man. A deep laceration appeared on his forehead and cuts and bruises covered his bare chest and arms. Having been stripped by the medical technician the young man had found a sheet to wrap around his waist. His eyes cast panicked glances from one end of the room to another as he held the blade up before him. With no hesitation, Marisol walked over the examination room door and nodded for the security guard to allow her to enter.

Taking a deep breath, she exhaled her laced-with-fear excitement when stepping inside.

Closing the door behind her, Marisol's voice sounded soft and soothing as she offered words of welcome.

"Hello. Buenos Dias. Bonjour." Knowing the young man had found refuge in the corner of the room, behind a supply cabinet, Marisol continued slowly walking in his direction until reaching the edge of the examination table. Stopping here, her eyes captured full view of him. "Is it possible you cannot speak?" she questioned aloud. "Have I failed to greet you with your proper language?"

Momentary silence was ended with three words uttered by him.

"I speak English."

With relief in knowing he could understand her, Marisol stepped closer. Her life's work had been based upon the studies of artifacts, theories, and historical references. Yet, having a live daylighter standing there, before her, made her feel most unprepared. It was also at this very moment when Marisol understood she would fail to be the same after this encounter. Never before had she been in the presence of such a handsome man. Only in textbooks had she studied dark hair such as his. His was what once was referred to as auburn and somewhat short in length with a few curls and waves. His skin was tanned to a light, golden, caramel shade. And she found herself instantly attracted to his muscular frame though his eyes, of such beautiful brown color, were what truly held her spellbound. The mere sight of them nearly robbed her of her breath.

Continuing to move with caution, Marisol approached him.

"Please...lower the blade. I give you my word that no harm will come to you." The young man stood motionless for a moment while staring at her. She noticed a subtle tremble in his hand as he lowered the blade slowly. Opening her palm, he tentatively placed the blade there. Then holding out her other hand, Marisol calmly urged him.

"Please follow me over to the table. I would like for you to sit so that I may tend to your injuries."

He hesitated, for a moment, before taking her hand and allowing her to lead him to the table. Once seated, she examined the laceration on his forehead. Concentration proved difficult for Marisol as he stared at her the entire time. His striking, brown eyes seemed to convey an array of emotions, from fear to sadness to confusion. How could eyes express so much at one time?

Reaching for a bottle on the table, Marisol poured a clear lotion onto her fingers.

"This may sting. My apologies. It is not my intention to cause you further discomfort," she whispered, to him. Soothingly, she covered the laceration with the lotion, taking notice to his slight wince when touching his wound. Seeing a single tear streaming from his eye, she swallowed hard when feeling it touch her finger, regretting deeply any pain she had caused.

Pouring more lotion on to her finger tip, she covered minor scratches on his hands before smoothing the lotion over scrapes and cuts on his chest. For a moment, her fingertips lingered there feeling the rapid beating of his heart and the muscles protecting it. Glancing up, her eyes met his startling her by the intensity of emotions his exuded. Looking away, unnerved by how he continued watching her, Marisol attempted to shift focus by attempting conversation.

"My name is Marisol. What is your name?"

"Sage." His voice held soothing depths to it unlike any she had heard before, offering no relief for her growing dilemma. How would she ever be able to objectively study the daylighter when so easily being drawn to him?

***

Dressing in clothes provided for him by her, each piece reminded him of clothing certain to be worn by a wealthy gentleman from the early, twentieth century. However, none perfectly fit him.

"The pants are a little too short and the shirt is too tight for me to button," Sage commented. "The jacket and vest are also probably going to be too small."

Having stepped away in letting him have some privacy, Marisol turned to him.

"I will see if I am able to locate clothing to better fit you. If not, I will consult with a tailor to fashion clothes to your specific needs. I also apologize for not finding shoes your size." She took a step away as if distracted.

"That's alright. I've never worn shoes before. It was always warm…at home." Touching her arm when finished dressing, she jumped, clearly startled by him. "I'm sorry. I didn't mean to scare you."

"No apology is necessary," she answered, while keeping her eyes from looking at him.

"May I ask you a question?"

"Of course! I am quite certain you have many," Marisol responded.

"Before my dad died, he used to be afraid of the dark, afraid of what was hidden within it. I think that he may have been wrong. I think that, maybe *you* are afraid of *me*. Are you?"

Noticing her startled expression and tense body language, Sage believed her answer would be yes, but she clearly denied this.

"Not at all," she lied, while forcing a smile on her face yet avoiding eye contact.

"Just out of curiosity, why are we dressed in Victorian era clothes?"

"How are you familiar with this?" Marisol asked, expressing disbelief with his correct recognition of the time period regarding their clothing.

"My mother taught me history when I was younger."

She was visibly impressed.

"It is wonderful that your education in history was so thorough. As for *why* we are dressed as we are, the Victorian Era is highly regarded in our society. There was a civility and sophistication within those times which our government wishes to emulate. Decades of social and moral decay, in many ways, has been viewed as a social downfall with subsequent generations. Our government sought the return of a classical age when society was not marred by the immoral, corrupt epidemic ushered in through generations tainted by toxic, social media components." Sage remained quiet while thinking about her answer, both confused and struck by how far this place had gone in seeking a return to the past.

"Please follow me. Arrangements have been made for a place for you to rest," Marisol offered, pulling him away from his thoughts.

Hesitant in trailing behind her when leaving the examination room, Sage noticed they were now alone, the men whom he first came in contact with having left. He followed her down a small brightly lit hallway until they reached a door at the end. Exposing an electronic security wristband to a wall sensor, the door silently slid open and Marisol walked inside.

"Will this be my prison cell?" Sage asked, stopping in the doorway while looking around. Clearly stunned by his question, Marisol struggled for a response. "You don't need to answer that. I understand."

The room proved rather spacious. The Victorian-styled furnishings including the large canopy bed, an ornately decorated sofa set near a fireplace, and a grandfather clock offered the appearance of comfort. The walls were painted a pale shade of gray and featured a plush, oriental carpet complimenting the color on the walls. Marisol stood off to the side as Sage explored the room. A lavatory with a white, claw-foot bathtub was off to the left. Sage instantly noticed the one thing the room lacked.

"There's no window. Is it because I might be frightened by what exists beyond these walls or would your people be frightened by me?"

Again, obviously unnerved by his question, Marisol instead shifted the conversation to a more comfortable and safe topic.

"You must be famished. I will have some food sent here for you."

"No. I'm not hungry." But after saying this, the audible, hunger contraction of his stomach muscles betrayed his answer.

Seeming discouraged and concerned that this offer of hospitality had been rejected, Marisol walked over to a small control panel on the wall.

"Here is something I sincerely hope will make your stay more pleasurable," she said, leaning her face close to the panel. "Winter." He barely heard the whisper. An expansive, white, frozen scene showing pine trees and snow-covered ground appeared across the walls and the floor. Then it began to snow. Sage's eyes grew large with wonder, finding no words to speak. Reaching his hand out to feel the snowflakes, each one disappeared when he touched them. "It is all a computer-generated illusion," Marisol offered. He heard her whisper "autumn." The scene changed to a forest of beautiful, multi-colored leaves of gold, crimson and orange. Sage once more reached out his hand as the leaves began to fall from the ceiling. And once again they disappeared when he tried touching them. Amazed by this, he noticed how relaxed Marisol had grown in sharing this with him.

"May I try?" he asked. Marisol smiled and stepped away. Sage walked over to the panel.

"Summer," Sage whispered. The autumn scenery faded away, being quickly replaced by a scene showing a beach and an ocean. White clouds drifted across the sky blue ceiling, majestically. Sage felt a strong breeze caress the skin on his cheek. "How is this possible?"

Marisol smiled.

"As I said before, it is a computer-generated illusion. We may live in the darkness but that does not mean we do not crave what we once had on Earth. The seasons are just as much a part of our lives now as they were years ago. The only difference is that we may now select which season we wish to be in, and change it randomly as our moods see fit."

"Night," Marisol whispered, stepping back from the panel. Plunged to darkness, the only light now shone was the soft glimmer of millions of stars covering the walls and ceiling. Too stunned to speak by what he was seeing, Sage glanced about at stars he had only seen pictures of when learning about them as a kid.

"Now is time for rest," Marisol offered. "Tomorrow I would very much like to return here and talk with you about your life as a daylighter, if that would be alright?"

Lured away from this night illusion by her question, Sage's heart sank in understanding what his future here held, to lead a life as both prisoner and experimental subject.

"I don't think I have a choice. Do I?"

Unexpectedly, Marisol responded with what Sage knew to be the truth.

"No. I do not believe you have a choice in this. Yet I would encourage you not to view all of this as a prison. In time, I hope you will embrace the opportunity for a new life here. There is *so much* we can offer you."

"Can you offer me my life back in the sunlight?"

"No," Marisol replied, glancing away startled by his question.

Chapter Four

Hours later, Marisol entered the room, growing distressed in noticing Sage missing. Continuing into the lavatory, she discovered him there and found herself unable to lure her eyes away from him. He had just finished bathing and was towel drying his wet body. Finally turning away, she understood how her attraction to him had intensified sending fear through her. When she glanced back at him, slightly, their eyes seemed to catch hold of each other before Sage lowered his.

Composing herself, she walked over to him.

"I would like to examine the laceration on your forehead. I promise to be gentle," she said. Wrapping the towel around his waist, Sage held still as she touched the wound soothingly to see how much it had healed overnight.

Concentrating on her task, Marisol struggled internally to focus, with Sage's eyes unrelenting in watching her. His breath felt warm against her neck, causing her to believe she was being tortured unintentionally. He was a threat to everything she knew and unlike anyone she had ever met. His beautiful, penetrating eyes expressed rampant emotions which left her both spellbound and concerned that her resistance to them would falter. His presence held a direct challenge to the sterile and controlled life all citizens of New London embraced with unflinching compliance.

Sage changed into some new clothes that Marisol had brought for him. These seemed to fit better.

"The shirt is made of silk," she commented. "I also brought you a pair of shoes for a time when we venture out into the city."

"I didn't think I'd be allowed to do that."

"You are not a prisoner," Marisol responded.

"The lock on the door seems to dispute that," Sage argued, politely, for which she had no answer.

She brushed off his reaction to her comment, and motioned for him to sit down on the edge of the bed next to her.

"You must have many questions that you would like to ask?"

"No. I just have one question for now."

"Well…what would that be?" Marisol uttered, attempting to hide a deep breath as fear inside her grew.

"Have you ever found any other daylighters?" Sage asked, with some hesitation.

Marisol let out her breath as their conversation would enter comfortable terrain.

"We have discovered remains, mostly skeletal or decomposed. You are the only daylighter we have ever captured alive." She recognized her poor selection of words, instantly. Sage looked with caution to her as she attempted damage control from her statement. "Please forgive me. I stand by my previous statement. I did not mean to insinuate *in any way* that you are a prisoner."

"I'm as good as one…and we both know it," he whispered, his tone brimming with sadness.

***

Through the course of the next several days, Marisol offered a history of what she referred to as the nightdwellers, herself included. She spoke of life on their orbiting city, New London, as well as four similar cities; New Atlanta, New Phoenix, New Columbia, and New Asia. Sage was provided with a history of how their societies came to be as well as the current, social structures. He seemed mildly interested for the most part.

"Why don't your cities all cluster together? Why are they so far away?"

For a moment Marisol thought about this. In all honesty she didn't have an answer for this question. And the more she gave thought to it the more troubled she felt. From time to time one city would encounter another, yet they would not stay together for more than a few weeks or at most a month. To her vast knowledge, there had never been a gathering of all of the cities at one time. Why was that?

After a moment of thought, she diverted the question back to Sage.

"Rumors of an armada of skyjammers have been spoken of for years. Does such an armada exist?"

Sage shrugged his shoulders.

"My mom talked about it but we never found it."

"Do you know of any other daylighters?"

"No. I never knew of anyone other than my parents. Sometimes we would hear words that our short-wave radios would pick up but we never met anyone else."

"Where are your parents?"

"They're gone," Sage responded. "What about you? Where are your parents?"

"According to my birth records, my father and mother live on New Atlanta. My mother is our ambassador to that city. My father is a genetics professor," Marisol responded.

"Birth records? I don't understand. Were you abandoned or given up for adoption?"

"No," she responded, plainly. "Children born on New London are sent to special academies shortly after birth. Parent-child bonds are never established. Education and technical training are paramount in our society."

"I'm sorry. I still don't understand."

"When a female citizen of New London reaches the age of twenty-five, after she is established in her career field, she may choose to be artificially inseminated in efforts to increase our population. There is a rigorous screening process to match the woman with a suitable sperm donor. Before the end of the first trimester, the fetus is surgically removed as gestation is continued in a clinical environment."

"Unbelievable," Sage mumbled. "But, then, how is it that you know who your parents are?"

"Through records of lineage obtained from our Parental Origin Database. None of these records are considered confidential. Most citizens select not to pursue access to this information as it is inconsequential."

"Inconsequential?"

"My apology; it means irrelevant."

"I understand what the word means," Sage responded, with more noticeable disbelief. "So you *never* bond with your parents. You *never* know what it is like to love them and be loved by them. You never know what it feels like when they're gone and you know you'll never see them again?"

"No," she responded. For the first time ever she actually felt slightly troubled by this. A moment of silence passed between them. "Do you miss your parents?"

"Yes."

"Why?"

"Because I loved them," Sage answered, and then looked away. Marisol, herself, looked away. Love was not a concept of which she had ever been permitted to study yet she wondered if she was being confronted by it at this very moment. Sage was all she could think about and she didn't want to stop. It was more than that. She knew she couldn't stop. For the first time she understood that possibly it was not yet *love* she was experiencing, but more likely attraction and obsession...with love lurking dangerously close.

***

Dragged out of bed from his arm being yanked on, Sage was about to say something when a hand covered his mouth.

"Please do not speak. They will hear you," Heroin whispered, faintly. "Remain low and follow me." She scooted under the bed frame.

Sage's eyes grew large when seeing her disappear through an air vent under his bed. Looking down, he saw a flicker of light inside of what appeared to be a metal air duct. Climbing in cautiously, he saw her holding a flashlight and motioning for him to crawl toward her. Feeling a rush of warm air, he kept pace with her as they made their way to an intersection. Turning right at the next intersection, they crawled left. After several minutes, they arrived at a large, open, air vent at the end of the air ducts.

Awkwardly climbing through, when standing up, Sage looked forward and then overhead at a staircase leading high up in what he thought to be a tower.

"Follow me," Heroin urged. After climbing several flights, Sage grew dizzy and sluggish as his legs began feeling weighed down. Glancing up, he sighed when realizing they were only half way up the tower. By the time they reached the top, through lightheadedness, he tried catching his breath as tremors coursed through his legs.

Emerging from the shadows, Sage's eyes enlarged when looking upon then mechanisms of a massive clock. Awed by immense gears turning with precision, he wandered about in fascination of their surroundings.

"This is incredible," he uttered. Noticing two large clock hands keeping time for the outside, he stepped over and gazed out through a small window. The star-lit night sky reminded him of the illusion Marisol had shown him in his room yet this view was far more stunning to behold. Sparks, from meteors colliding with the atmosphere, corrupted an expanse of stars seeming without end. He thought it might be the most beautiful thing he'd ever seen.

Hearing movement from below, his jaw dropped when watching a steam engine speeding along what he thought were elevated, tram tracks constructed to appear as old time rails. The architecture of the white-colored buildings appeared authentic even with modern elements subtly included. To Sage, all seemed to be a blending of vintage and futuristic styles. Great care had been given to reinvent the past, much like the clothing he'd been given to wear.

"What is this place?" he uttered, lost to its wonder.

"This is a replication of Big Ben," Lord Amphetamine answered, appearing from the opposite side of the clock. Backing away toward the corner, Sage's movement proved obvious. "I humbly request your forgiveness in having Lithium knock you unconscious," Lord Amphetamine begged. "When seeing the white city approaching, I was uncertain you would willingly assist us in keeping our hiding aboard your skyjammer a secret. You have my word. It shall never happen again."

"I guess I understand. Otherwise we'd *all* be their prisoners, instead of just me," Sage responded, wearily.

"For us, it would have been far worse, my friend."

"How?"

He watched Lord Amphetamine pass concerned glances to Heroin, Adrenaline and Lithium.

"All of us once dwelled here in the white city until we were banished."

"You mean…you used to *live* here?"

"Yes."

"But…why would they banish you?"

"We were deemed a stain on the fabric of their proper society," Lord Amphetamine confessed. "Before our banishment, our very existence proved vulgar and profane by the elite due to our failings. As you will come to find, while lingering here in the white city, though some have embraced and mastered the technological progress surrounding them humans remain a flawed component in the design of a world striving for perfect." He wandered over to the others. "At one time each one of us surrendered who we were to a demon known by the name *addiction.* The four of us have now assumed the identity of that which we surrendered ourselves to as reminders in our vigilance to never more fall prey to the seductive lure our addictions held. For me, it was the abuse of amphetamines. For our lovely, Evangeline, her demon was heroin. Brendan, here, sought new highs with his addiction to adrenaline and Richard fought valiantly against manic episodes, aggression, hyperactivity, and depression until tasting the forbidden fruit of lithium. Others here in the white city have suppressed and concealed their own addictions and obsessions. Some prove easier to hide than others. For us, we held no such success with this. And, as for the city elite, they selected to banish the four of us rather than offering assistance in relieving us the burdens of our addictions."

"Why wouldn't they help you?"

"The answer to this question will be revealed, all in good time, yet time is not our ally with this endeavor. You, my friend, must return to your room now until we meet again."

"No, *please*, let me stay with you," Sage pleaded.

Smiling, Lord Amphetamine walked over to Sage and firmly grasped his shoulders.

"Soon, my friend but, for now, we need you to act as a distraction. With the elite's eyes feasting on watching your every move, *rats*…such as us can move freely in our efforts to expose the most terrible of addictions."

"And what would that be?"

"Lies, my friend. One leading to another and another." Lord Amphetamine remarked, extending his arms out. "All this you see before you is much like a beautiful tower built of cards. At first glance, the structure appears sturdy, yet this is no more than a fallacy, a lie. And, within this structure, is hidden a joker; a foolish imposter assuming his place among the elite while falsely projecting an image of power. It is him we seek and, once exposed, his lies will fall unleashing a truth so well hidden."

Chapter Five

After crawling back under his bed from inside the air duct, Sage turned around to look at Heroin. Smiling at him, she then unexpectedly leaned forward, placing a soft kiss on his lips.

"Why did you do that?" he whispered.

"I have wanted nothing else but to do that from the first moment I saw you," she responded. "May I ask your name, before we part, kind sir?"

"Sage."

"Meaning one venerated for wisdom," Heroin commented. "A much better name than my own."

"Maybe you should change your name," he suggested. "By adding an *e* to the end of it, your name would change to *Heroine*, meaning a woman greatly admired for her bravery." A beaming smile lit her expression when hearing this.

"Thank you," she responded to his kind remark. As she moved to leave him, Sage stopped her by offering his own soft kiss to her lips. Caressing her cheek, he noticed her smile grow even bigger. "Now I regret the need to part from you even more."

"Maybe you'll want to come back to see me," Sage suggested.

"I would very much like that," she said, before disappearing.

Hearing his door opening, Sage quickly scooted out from under the bed but stayed hidden there on the floor. Seeing Marisol rush into sight, Sage watched her place her hands over her chest.

"I am so relieved! I saw you missing from your bed and worried about you. Why are you lying here on the floor?"

"I was scared," Sage answered, thinking fast, while glancing away from her.

"Of what?"

"Everything," he responded, clutching his blanket close to him.

Kneeling at his feet, Marisol tried comforting him.

"No one here will hurt you. You are safe. Please, believe me."

"How…did you know I wasn't in bed?" Sage sat up, and asked, acting as if he'd just realized he was being watched.

"Well…I…," Marisol stammered, appearing started by his question.

"Are you watching me?" he continued, faking shock. "Are there surveillance cameras in here, watching everything I do? There is. Isn't there?"

"Please, I beg you to understand—."

"Understand what?" Sage interrupted. "That I'm a dangerous prisoner needing watched every minute or a science experiment you want to keep track of."

Please leave me alone." Rolling over, he glanced under the bed while staying quiet. A minute later, he heard Marisol stand and then heard his door close.

***

Hours later when again hearing Marisol enter his room, Sage keep his eyes watching the simulated flames in the fireplace rather than looking at her.

"Good morning," she greeted, with Sage noticing tension in her tone.

"I didn't realize it was morning," he responded. "Maybe if my prison cell had windows I might have known. No wait! It's always night here. Never mind."

"I would like you to come with me," she invited him. "I have arranged for you to tour one of our city's finest landmarks."

"Why bother?"

"You are *not* a prisoner," Marisol insisted. "New London could be your home, a new beginning for you. I very much wish to share with you one of my favorite places. *Please.*"

Reluctantly, Sage stood up. When doing so, he saw how the anxiousness cast over her expression lightened.

"Lead the way."

Stepping outside, Sage glanced up at the stars shining through a clear glass dome covering the city. Antique lit streetlamps, though, corrupted their brilliance, robbing the night sky of its darkness. Feeling the coolness of the cobblestone path under his bare feet, Sage inhaled deeply, smelling purified air holding a sterile quality to it, yet almost natural.

As he followed her, Sage fell under staring glances from many people, seeming more curious about him than fearful. Each man and woman had pale complexions and light-colored hair. They were also dressed in fashions from the Victorian era, yet were communicating on cell phones and miniature devices on their wrists and in their ears. In each direction he looked, Sage found evidence of the false authenticity New London exuded. Everything appeared as a well-thought-out lie.

"I guess I'm confused in seeing so many people with personal communication devices. I thought you said social media was banned?"

"The citizenry of New London has full access to a central information authority. Only government sanctioned messages are posted on this one site. Each man and woman is assigned a personal communication device. While texting and direct communication with other is permitted, all is strictly monitored with severe repercussions for those in violation of regulations and moral conduct."

"What kind of *repercussions*?"

"A lifetime ban for use of personal communication devices, counseling, and social reorientation for those in violation."

"Kind of like reprogramming a computer?"

"In a manner of speaking," Marisol agreed. "I recognize the parallels with this."

"What about robots? Are they used here?"

"All technology, robotics included, is embraced here, yet extensively controlled. The common citizenry is provided technological access deemed appropriate for their circumstance, with laborers and artisans holding the least access and scientists, the government elite, and skill professions such as physicians holding significantly more."

"To our right, you will see both the men's and women's dormitories," Marisol pointed out.

"Married couples don't live together?" Sage asked.

"Marriage is forbidden in our society."

"Any chance you have a library close by devoted to George Orwell?" Sage uttered, sarcastically.

"My apology, I am not familiar with his literature."

"I didn't think you would be."

Approaching a large white building having three massive glass domes, when stepping inside, Sage's eyes enlarged with wonder in seeing the unimaginable.

"What is this place?"

"To our right, you will find the botanical gardens. Ahead of us is the metropolitan aquarium. And to our left, you will see the zoological menagerie. Which would you prefer to tour first?"

Without answering, Sage walked forward into a glass tunnel. Awestruck when softly touching his fingers to the clear surface, he watched an array of tropical fish and sea horses swim past him. Above a jagged multi-colored coral reef and swaying anemones, a great white shark circled amidst a school of stingrays. Glancing in the opposite direction, Sage smiled when seeing playful dolphins, sea turtles and a black and white orca passing by. And when looking toward the bottom of the view in front of him, Sage watched a lionfish and sea urchins disturb an octopus from its hiding place. Having studied these creatures on his computer when growing up, he never thought a day would come when being in their living presence.

"This is *amazing*! How were you able to preserve these incredible creatures?"

"Through animatronics," Marisol answered.

"Through...*what*?" Sage uttered, stunned by her answer.

"Animatronics," she matter-of-factly responded. "Regretfully, none of what you are viewing is real. Every creature in sight has been fabricated through animatronics. In each, robotic devices are employed to emulate lifelike characteristics."

Stepping back from the glass, Sage wandered away. Entering the zoological menagerie, his eyes remained large, marveling in watching a giraffe wander majestically near a lion and spotting a herd of undisturbed zebras surrounding an elephant. Noticing a chimpanzee step close to the class barrier, when closely studying it, Sage couldn't find a single trace of its robotics. All its movements and mannerisms appeared flawless and natural, just like all the other animals. But his heart sank, knowing none of this was real. Everything is sight was a lie.

"Are the plants and flowers fake too?" he asked, leaving the menagerie and entering through the doorway of the botanical garden.

"No. Every plant, tree and flower is authentic. The botanical garden assists with the purification of our air here in New London." Breathing in the fragrances of flowers near him, Sage believed she was telling the truth with this.

"So, the plants are real, but the animals aren't."

"*These* particular animals are not," Marisol confirmed. "There is an area devoted to genetically enhanced livestock and fowl, used for eating consumption."

"And…what about the people here, the citizens of New London, are they real?"

"*Of course!*" she answered, with obvious dismay.

"Are you sure?" Appearing flustered in hearing him asks this, Marisol turned away.

***

Carrying a silver tray in serving his dinner, Marisol noticed how little of his lunch had been eaten, especially the meat not having been touched. Concerned Sage wasn't consuming enough calories she'd made numerous attempts to introduce a variety of foods and beverages for him to try. However, he drank only water and ate only certain fruits and vegetables while refusing to try anything other than what he'd eaten before.

"Why does fire hold such enchantment for you?" Once more finding him sitting near the fireplace, staring at the flames.

"Because it reminds me of the sun. It reminds me of home. Nothing else here does."

"Were you interested, you could accompany me to my laboratory at the Cultural Ministry," she suggested. "I have a collection of daylighter artifacts that might interest you. We could venture there now…if you would like."

"Do you consider me one of your artifacts?"

"No," she uttered, hoping she'd sounded convincing despite pausing her answer.

"Alright, lead the way."

When stepping inside the nearby train station, Marisol watched Sage's expression of astonishment. First glancing up at the cathedral-height frosted glass ceiling, his eyes then fixed on the replicated steam engine pulling up to the platform. She felt spellbound when seeing him smile as steam pillowed from the engine, causing butterflies in her stomach. This left her wondering if when leading his life in the sunlight was he always this happy? If only she could find a way to make him happy here.

"This is remarkable!" he uttered. "Does the train use electro-magnetic technology to glide on the rails?"

"Yes, very much so." Marisol answered, again, his high level of intelligence impressed her.

Finding seats in the silver passenger coach, Marisol studied his amazed reactions to sites outside his window when traveling to the Cultural Ministry. Sage acted like a child first exposed to the wonders of the world. But thinking back to her youth, she tried recalling a moment when she felt the same way and grew disturbed when not one memory presented itself.

Upon arrival, Marisol spotted Governor Valorian leaving. Yet, his reaction when seeing her and Sage together proved distressing to her by the sternness of his expression. Having spent so much time with him in the past, in seeing Valorian forcing a grin she understood the admonishment lurking behind this façade. Seldom had she ever suffered such from him but would now taste the bitter fruit of his displeasure.

"My dearest, Marisol, I *see* you have selected to abandon protocol with regards to our *guest*."

"It is my wish to further our research by bringing Sage here to the ministry…to shed light on some artifacts I have struggled to catalogue," she responded, attempting to remain composed.

"What kind of protocols has she abandoned?" Sage interjected into their conversation.

"Until such time when you have been thoroughly instructed with the conventions and principles of our society, you…our *esteemed* guest…pose a distraction with your *free-spirited* ideals," Valorian answered while glancing at Sage's unbuttoned shirt and bare feet.

"His indoctrination into our society has already begun. There remain a few components which require further progress. He has proven an apt pupil…and will excel under my tutelage."

"I should hope so," Valorian retorted, firmly. "Good day to you both."

After watching him walk away, Marisol turned her attention back to Sage, who was staring at her. Unsure of what to say, he rescued her from this dilemma.

"We should go inside. I don't want you to get in any more trouble," he suggested.

"Yes, of course."

***

Entering her laboratory, Sage had expected a cold sterile environment. But everything in sight held direct contrast to this. Overhead coffered ceiling featuring exposed wood beams complimented the hardwood floors and walls of bookshelves. An ornately carved mantle surrounded the fireplace, though with simulated flames within the grate. At the room's center, a large, wood table sat littered with objects Sage instantly recognized.

Wandering closer, he picked up an old short-wave radio similar to the one they had on their skyjammer. He then noticed a brass telescope. Picking it up, he held it as if finding a unique treasure from long ago. But then he saw something jaw-dropping among the clutter. Reaching out, his fingers traced over a gold medallion attached to a chain. Carved into its surface was a rendering of the sun. Placing it in his palm, for the longest time he stared at it until her question broke this trance. "What is the significance of that?"

"My dad used to wear this around his neck. Where did you find it?"

Walking over to the far end of the table, Marisol fetched a small cedar box and brought it over to him. "Several years ago, this was discovered among the wreckage of another skyjammer. Inside this box is its twin, along with three metal toy soldiers and a black and white photograph of three young boys. You are welcome to look through this if you would like."

Taking the box from her, at first Sage hesitated in opening the lid. But after doing so, his heart nearly stopped when staring at a picture taken of three boys standing near a hot air balloon. And with his hand shaking, Sage turned it over and silently read the handwritten names on the back: *Luke, Wyatt,* and *Caleb*.

Chapter Six

Having spent a few hours answering Marisol's inquiries regarding artifacts salvaged from derelict skyjammers, further questions began probing deeper into his former life. Reliving these moments caused him to have feelings of sadness in longing for days spent in the sunlight with his parents. Although some memories of his dad seemed clouded with many things forgotten, he remembered as if it was yesterday sitting on his dad's lap at the helm, feeling the coarseness of his whiskers against his cheek. And he remembered tracing his fingers over the engraved sun on the medallion his dad wore around his neck.

Memories of his mother remained fresh in his mind. Sage recalled when listening to their shortwave radio how she'd reminisce about songs once played on radios. She'd tell him stories of when she was growing up on Nantucket Island and Cape Cod. As much as she talked about his dad missing the wide open spaces of Nebraska, she equally missed walking along shore of the ocean, leaving Sage wishing he could have seen both places.

"Since leaving my laboratory, you have remained most quiet. I sense something is troubling you and I would like to offer my help…if I am able," Marisol offered, when returning to his room.

"Unless you can somehow find a time machine that would let me go back to my life in the sunlight…then I doubt anything you could do will help me. I'm just having a hard time adjusting to the fact for the rest of my life all I'll ever be is one of your daylighter artifacts pretending not to be a prisoner. But the thing I find even more disturbing…is that I'm not the only prisoner here."

"I fail to understand your theory of this. There are no prisoners here in New London," Marisol insisted.

"You're wrong. From what you've explained to me, every one of you is being held captive and everything around you is a lie. But I'm not surprised you can't see the truth."

"I challenge you to provide proof of this," she argued, the agitation in her tone evident.

Pressing his hand against the fireplace screen, Sage then removed it, revealing no burns to her.

"I don't feel a thing, like everyone else here."

"You *wished* to be scorched by the flames?"

"Don't *you*? Don't you wish to feel *something*? Sage asked.

"I assure you, all citizens, myself included, hold the capacity for showing emotions. Yet our society refrains from outbursts of such as deemed inappropriate in public settings. New London is a vibrant metropolis brimming with well-educated professionals leading content-filled lives."

"I doubt that. Just look around you," he urged, quietly. "Everything in sight is flawlessly disguised, including the citizens of your *vibrant* utopia. From what I've witnessed, those in power here have created a false world, a synthetic society floundering within a stagnant social climate. And the people here have yielded, blindly, all freedoms and liberties to dystopian and totalitarian principles. Every man, woman, and child here has surrendered."

"Surrendered what?"

"Their passion and freedom of thought, their zeal for life, their individuality and creativity," Sage responded. "When we were outside, I watched the people, each one having vacant expressions while blankly staring off or at the screens on their communication devices. They spoke in murmurs and not once did I hear any traces of laughter or see anyone even smile. You claim that no one here is a robot. Maybe physically, that's true. But when people surrender their right to express emotions and think and speak freely for themselves, they're no better than hollow machines. That's why they're prisoners...and that's the future you want me to embrace."

For the first time, seeing her face red with anger, he wondered if she'd ever truly felt this emotion before. In no way did he regret forcing this reaction from her, understanding how Marisol needed to be confronted with real emotions buried deep inside her. Seeing her storming away to the door, Sage expected her to leave. But gripping the handle, for a few minutes she stared at the door's fake wood surface and then surprised him when tracing her fingers over the grains as if testing to see if it was real. The torrent from her anger then appeared to subside when she released a deep exhale while timidly glancing over.

Watching Marisol kneel down next to him, Sage noticed the confusion on her expression as she struggled to find something to say.

"Why are you sad?" Sage asked, seeing a tear stream down her cheek.

"Because, with my deepest regrets, no argument on my part could dispute this. Every word you spoke is the truth, a theory I have understood yet fought against for the longest time. Each morning when I look at me reflection in the mirror I am confronted by this reality." Studying her hands, she continued, "From my earliest memories, all aspects of my life have been dictated for me, from how to dress to carriage and demeanor. This holds true for all other citizen as well. The principle philosophies of our nightdweller society are discipline, unflinching conformity, and the undisputed theory that logic is perfection. Variables such as love and hate, influencing happiness and sadness, are deemed corruptive and are eradicated whenever they manifest in behaviors. People within our society have been educated to ignore these variables. To lead with one's heart or be seduced by dark thoughts and subjugate the logical mind is to travel a path ultimately leading to self-destruction. The power elite time and again have warned of love's foolish imperfection and the seductive recklessness of hatred. Hearts full of love can be so easily misled, following impulsive thoughts to disastrous results, rendering them broken beyond repair. As for hatred, to look upon the toxic wasteland that is now Earth is enough of a reminder for anyone to fathom its corrupt power. Before your arrival, like others I blindly followed this path, the only path ever presented to me."

"And now?"

"I have been confronted with the error of my thinking. Since your arrival, I have succumbed to a madness I never dreamed the affliction of. You...have become my obsession, an addiction I hold no theory in how to cure. I find my heart beating faster when near you and aching to be with you when away. Never have I been drawn to anyone as I am drawn to you. In essence, your presence renders me your captive, a prisoner...as you have suggested."

Unexpectedly, Sage felt stunned when Marisol leaned over and kissed his lips while caressing his cheek. But before he could think of a response, the lights from the overhead chandelier and crystal table lamps extinguished, plunging the room into darkness.

"What's going on?"

"I am not certain," Marisol uttered, in confusion.

Appearing on the wall next to the door, to both their surprise a black and white film began showing. Standing up, they watched rapid vintage images of New London set against the celestial background. Sage recognized many of the sites, from the train station to the botanical garden to the replication of Big Ben. There were also places he hadn't seen, academies where children learned, physicians caring for patients in a hospital, and an auditorium crowded with people listening to a lecture.

Images of citizens performing skilled labor then appeared. Each person clearly shone discipline and conformity while lacking visible traces of happiness or contentment. Their vacant facial expressions confirmed all confessed by Marisol.

With the film seeming to have ended, Marisol walked over to the voice activation panel to terminate its showing.

"End motion picture transmission," she instructed.

But, the program failed to respond to her verbal command. New images began appearing on the wall, with Sage's eyes enlarging with shock. Standing paralyzed, he felt bewildered at first when watching the distorted pictures until through improving clarity all he saw turned grotesque. Scene after scene depicted the capturing of skyjammers and the brutal detainments of daylighters. The high-pitched volume of interrogating questions and frantic answers forced Sage in falling to his knees while covering his ears. Far worse images of profane and sadistic experimentations of daylighters were followed with maddening laughter at vulgar and deplorable exploitations. "Stop this!" Sage shouted, covering his face with his hands when bursting to tears.

"Terminate program! Terminate program!" Marisol tearfully screamed into the voice activation panel. Even when pounding on the screen, the program continued defying her commands.

Feeling Marisol try comforting him, Sage pushed her away, his body convulsing with fear. The ear-splitting volume then instantly lowered. With his chest heaving in trying to calm his rampant breathing, when spying through his fingers, Sage saw himself and Marisol now on screen. Every word spoken between them from the moment they returned to his room sounded out with the final scene showing her leaning over and kissing him.

"Sage," she whispered, faintly. "I—."

"Leave," he exhaustedly uttered. "Please...leave."

Seeing her ghostly-white face expressing a vacant stare, Sage watched her stagger over to the door and wait for a moment before leaving. Once gone, he shakenly crawled over to his bed and then disappeared underneath.

***

"Everything will be *alright*. We were dispatched here to assist you." Stumbling in shock down the hallway, Marisol encountered two men dressed in white uniforms. The taller of the two spoke to her.

"With...what?" she responded, in a daze.

"Violations of moral conduct and seditious utterances," the shorter man answered.

Fighting through her clouded thoughts to regain her sense, these words confused her.

"I...fail...to...understand."

"All will be made clear upon your arrival at the reeducation ministry," the taller man said. "For your safety, we require your compliance in wearing this protective garment. Do be a dear and assist us in dressing you with it." Blankly nodding her head, Marisol allowed the men to restrain her arms inside a pure white straight jacket.

***

Slowly climbing one step after another, Sage's hand severely shook while gripping the metal railing. A few times his eyesight blurred from stinging tears. The dryness of his throat and panting from rampant breaths left him lightheaded. Staggering up the final few steps, from out of the shadows Sage wandered past the clock mechanisms to find a corner where he collapsed and then pulled his knees up to his chest, cowering in fear.

Seeing shadowed movements, Sage shuddered with fright when feeling someone softly caress his cheek.

"What has happened?" Heroin whispered.

Vacantly staring about, unable to focus, Sage wanted to scream but his throat had constricted so tightly not even a mumble could escape. The vile images he'd seen continued flashing in his mind, causing him to bury his face in his hands, silently begging them to stop.

"He suffers with shock," Sage heard Adrenaline say, through his fogged thoughts. He felt a blanket being eased over his legs and up his shoulders.

"Please, my dearest Sage, find your way out of the dark memory catacombs you have sought refuge within. It is such a hostile place where I cannot find you," Heroin begged.

"They…tortured…them."

"Who, my dearest?" she asked.

"I know of what he speaks of and has seen. I know of what has been done. I was there," Lithium answered for him. Quaking from hearing this revelation, Sage watched as tears streamed down Lithium's cheeks with Adrenaline consoling him.

"Do not speak of this," Adrenaline urged.

"I know what you saw, the profane nightmarish images," Lithium continued, brushing off Adrenaline's request. "Always, will I suffer the guilt of standing by and allowing the horrors to befall those innocent souls? Time and again I sought reprieve from that I bear witness to in many an attempt to end my life. Yet I proved too much of a coward to slash my wrists or hang from a noose. So I succumbed to the seduction of addiction to numb my torture." Glancing around, his eyes enlarged in fear, Lithium burst out while sobbing. "The white city is Satan's realm. The devils walk among us. We are all both prisoners and prey to their evil."

The sound of movements hidden within the shadows alerted them all to another's presence. Yet louder movements drew their attention toward the staircase. Sage's eye grew large when seeing the whitely-dressed image of a tall man step into the light, followed by several security guards carrying chains and armed with what appeared to be tasers and batons.

"Well…well…what have we here?" Valorian questioned, with a broad smirk.

Chapter Seven

Pushed along the quiet, streetlamp-lit, cobblestone streets when arriving at their destination Marisol looked confusingly at the white façade of Remington House, a place she had only heard of but never ventured near. With the fog in her mind clearing, shudders of fear coursed through her restrained body when realizing the men had brought her here to the New London Re-education Ministry. Though she had never met anyone forced to endure society reorientation instruction, whispered rumors of intense, therapeutic sessions cast a hushed aura of dread among the citizenry over this place.

Entering the building, they were greeted by a physician and nurse, both dressed in white.

"Good evening, Marisol. My name is Doctor Hiram Leetchworth and this is Nurse Miriam Jasper. It has come to our attention that you are in violation of moral and sedition protocols. That is why you have been escorted here. Do you understand these charges brought against you?"

Unable to speak out of fright, Marisol blankly stared away, her mind tormented with what would come next for her, as well as concerns for Sage's safety.

"Miriam, please lead Marisol through the ward to the examination room on the second floor," Doctor Leetchworth instructed, turning to the nurse.

Holding her breath, Marisol watched the doctor unlock a set of doors in front of them. Then being pushed slowly in her wheelchair by the nurse, they enter into what Marisol could only imagine to be a reflection of hell. Numerous patients chained to their beds lined a long dimly-lit ward, the walls and floors dark grey in color. Breathing in the pungent stench of human feces tainted with lye soap, Marisol felt nauseous as she attempted to shield her nose against the fabric of her straight jacket. Yet she could not lure her eyes away from the wretched souls trapped within this madness. Some of the men and women, both young and old, had succumbed to hysterical fits of sobbing and wailing while drowning out the insane murmurs of others. Several cast off vacant expressions while two aggressively tested the strength of the chains restraining them.

To Marisol, it seemed that Nurse Jasper was purposely pushing her wheelchair slow in passing by these patients. Was this a warning or threat should she fail in atoning for her committed crimes?

Intending to close her eyes to this horror, Marisol noticed a man at the far end of the ward stepping forward yet held back by his chained arms. Haggard and disheveled in appearance, the calmness expressed in his voice contrasted to the mania the others suffered.

"What crime have you committed?" he asked. Too frightened to offer a response, when being wheeled by him he confessed, "I told her I loved her…and I would tell her this a thousand times more and die a happy man in having done so." Backing away, he sat down on his bed, staring off in silence.

Once through the doors, the nurse pushed Marisol's wheelchair up to a lift, resembling a cage due to its many iron bars. Taking in anxious shallow breaths, the anticipation of what she would see next proved an insanity all its own. Feeling her stomach drop when ascending to the next floor, the ride up seemed both conflictingly endless yet regrettably short. With the doors parting in allowing them access to the second floor, Marisol held her breath, knowing how unprepared she would be for the devilry waiting here.

Again believing their pace was deliberately slow, one open door after the next revealed the terror lurking inside.

"These rooms are utilized when reeducation and reorientation therapies have failed," Nurse Jasper confirmed. "For some of our more *challenged* patients who fail wellness through prescribed medications and psychoanalytical treatments our neurologists are forced to employ vastly more intense therapies to cure disobedience. Lobotomies, electro-shock therapy, hydrotherapy, and even the use of skull spikes to relieve cranial pressure are practiced. Some may view these procedures as barbaric, yet to allow these poor souls to suffer with delusional and nonconforming behaviors…would be a crime unto itself. Hopefully your indiscretions of morality and sedition will not lead to such extreme measures." Nurse Jasper's last words, again, left Marisol with the impression as more of a threat than a genuine concern for her wellbeing.

Seeing a comfortably-furnished office to their right, Marisol anticipated being pushed inside. However, Nurse Jasper turned her in the opposite direction, wheeling her into a cold sterile examination room.

"The doctor will be in shortly for your reeducation assessment," she confirmed, to Marisol, before leaving her there alone. Glancing at the polished, white-tiled walls and floors, and observing an examination table and tray displaying several, medical instruments, her fear ran rampant in believing the worst would soon commence.

***

Arriving the same time as Governor Valorian and his security force and staying hidden in the shadows near the clock mechanism, Lord Amphetamine watched as his friends were bound in chains and shackles before being led away. With stealth, he followed them from the tower into a dark labyrinth of tunnels under the cobblestone streets.

While breathing in a light industrial odor, he felt noticeable rumblings under his feet from the nuclear reactors' powering anti-gravity thrusters enabling the city to hover above the Earth's surface as well as maintaining a constant speed in orbit.

Having traveled through these tunnels numerous times when sneaking around the city, Lord Amphetamine guessed where his friends were being taken, striking fear in his heart for their safety. Those few who had survived the harsh reeducation therapies at Remington House were never quite the same, appearing drained of life as mere shells of their former selves. This held especially true for Lithium, a former soldier driven to depression and suicidal thoughts in witnessing carnage he sparingly shared the memories of. It was from Remington House where Lord Amphetamine had rescued him from being beaten to death by the orderlies.

Hearing noise at his feet, glancing down he spotted a rat scampering along the wall, possibly the only animal in New London not animatronic or genetically engineered. Refocusing his attention on the scrapping of shoes ahead of him, Lord Amphetamine addressed the challenge he'd face when arriving at Remington House. Knowing the underground level was infested with rats, rather than following his friends and Governor Valorian, he instead chose to follow his small rodent companion, believing its way in would not be guarded.

Noticing the dim light fading, Lord Amphetamine continued on in blinding darkness until seeing a thin shaft of light penetrating from overhead. With one hand covering his mouth and nose from the stomach-turning stench of urine and feces, reaching out his other hand he grasped a lower rung of a metal ladder and began climbing up a cylinder-like passage. Hearing weeping and severe words of reprimand, Lord Amphetamine pushed up on a manhole covering, finding the washroom when spying out. Once certain he could sneak in unnoticed, easing the covering off to the side, he climbed out and scurried away to hide behind a storage cabinet.

Peeking out, Lord Amphetamine witnessed several naked patients being bathed by orderlies. Watching each one cowering in corners from harsh treatments, he wished to extract revenge on the orderlies, yet there was no time. Wondering how he could sneak away to find his friends, the answer to this appeared when a man dressed in a white uniform approached the storage cabinet. In failing to see him standing there, Lord Amphetamine held the advantage, surprising the man and knocking him unconscious. Dragging the orderly away and stripping him, Lord Amphetamine, pulled the man's uniform on over his clothes. Stepping out from his hiding place, he found a cart of supplies to push away, acting now as if an orderly making a delivery.

Leaving the washroom, he preceded on down a long hallway to a room at the far end, one seldom used. Intuition told him this was where his friends would be brought. In touching the door handle, Lord Amphetamine found the entrance locked. Peering in through a dirty glass window, feelings of dread washed over him in witnessing the punishment his friends now faced.

***

Forced by the security guards to strip off their clothing, Sage, Heroin, Adrenaline and Lithium waited for further instructions. "Each of you will dress in these uniforms provided for you." Valorian demanded, standing next to a long, metal table

Prodded to step forward, Sage looked at the oddly designed uniforms, wondering their purpose. He heard Lithium mumble under his breath.

"I know what this is." Sage looked first at him and then to Valorian, who expressed a wicked grin while standing there.

"Let Sage go," Adrenaline pleaded. "He has committed no crimes."

"His mere existence is a crime," Valorian argued. Glancing at Lithium, he continued, "Richard, have you found the courage to confess to your new friend your role in the capture and subsequent genocide of the daylighter population? You, by far, were one of our most dedicated soldiers…until your conflicted conscience betrayed your resolve to continue."

Watching tears streaming down Lithium's cheeks, Sage felt sad for his friend, the remorse of his actions evident. Drawn away, Sage fell under Valorian's stare.

"Were you ever curious as to why you never found the armada? I could easily burden you with the tragic details of the final days of the daylighter population, yet the images shown earlier to you reveal all. *You*…may very well be the last daylighter, such a distinction to have. Both you and Richard share a fellowship of the few alive who have witnessed their last sorrowful hours.

Seeing Lithium's jaw hanging low, this revelation clearly jarred him.

"Why? What did they do to cause you to be so cruel and evil?" Sage asked.

"Their continued existence threatened ours," Valorian confessed. "The citizenry of our great metropolis, while aware of our fascination and studies with regards to daylighter culture, have never been burdened with the knowledge of *decisions* made pertaining to the daylighter population. In addition, with efforts to conceal our doctrine of self-preservation, all soldiers holding both knowledge and having taken part in the detainment and euthanizing of the daylighter population…were terminated. All were *unfortunately* exposed to a viral strain causing death within days. Quarantined, their bodies were then cremated in efforts to thwart an epidemic."

With Lithium appearing in struggling to breathe, Adrenaline comfortingly held his friend's shuddering body close.

"You are a monster!" Adrenaline rasped, glaring.

"No," Valorian disagreed. "I am a god, shielding and protecting those who worship me. Not only have I cleansed the sky of the daylighter stain, I have also seen to the destruction of the other nightdweller cities as they too proved dangerous to our very survival. Think of New London as an ark, and me assuming the role of a benevolent lord, washing away sin to preserve purity. And with the overwhelming knowledge that the true God has turned his back on that which he had created, I shall fill the void left by him."

"What you see before you are unique uniforms fashioned in the spirit of what aviators and soldiers once donned in the First World War. In addition, each uniform is also provided with a helmet featuring a gas mask breathing apparatus, a small air tank containing enough oxygen for an hour, and a parachute. I encourage you to dress...*now*."

Feeling his heart in his throat and his pulse surging having no other option Sage followed Valorian's command in dressing in this strange uniform. With his chest anxiously heaving, when pulling on the gas mask and helmet he unsteadily staggered a step until breathing in the cold oxygen. Glancing at the others, they each held fear in their eyes for what would come next.

"Now, I understand what your initial thoughts were when brought here. I assure you, Remington House is not a place of execution, but rather a facility for reeducation, re-indoctrination, and when all else fails, a gate to exile." He pointed at Heroin, Adrenaline, and Lithium. "You three once before were exiled...*yet*...you found your way back. Therefore, I am left with no alternative other than to banish you to the only remaining place of exile. Should each of you survive your descent to the Earth's surface, it is my hope your deaths arrive quickly. *In fact*, if presented with such a dilemma, one might select to not even bother deploying the parachute…as impact would almost certainly summon instant death, sparing you from wasting your final moments on a world already dead."

Before Sage and the others could react, the floor underneath them opened, leaving them falling down a dark shaft.

Chapter Eight

Paralyzed with fear in seeing his friend's fall when the floor opened under them, while too stunned to look away, Lord Amphetamine watched the celebratory comradery among Valorian's security guards. Yet this moment's bravado came to a ghastly halt when Valorian raised a black semi-automatic rifle and repeatedly shot each guard, their bloodied bodies slumping to the floor, a few convulsing before stilled by death. With his held breath rushing from his lungs, Lord Amphetamine staggered back, lightheadedly glancing about in no longer recognizing where he was. Slouching down behind a laundry cart, he pulled his knees close to his chest as he stared away.

Vaguely noticing the room's door opening, he heard the sounds of clinking metal from something tossed into the laundry cart next to him. Summoning the courage to unsteadily stand, glancing down at the soiled sheets, Lord Amphetamine found Heroin's many necklaces discarded there, along with a sun-engraved medallion attached to a chain. Grasping all, he forced them into his pockets as his mind regained clarity. Looking through the dirty window one last time, he was startled to find the bodies of the security guards missing. Noticing the trap-doored floor closing, he guessed that Valorian had pushed the dead out and down to a final resting place on the Earth's surface.

With his only thought now of escaping from here, Lord Amphetamine spied around, reasoning over of his options. Remembering where he had entered Remington House, he looked over there and silently cursed when seeing the orderlies too near this passage in the floor. Thinking that since he had on a white uniform like the others he might slip out the front door unnoticed, taking a deep breath, he wandered away in search of that exit.

Dashing up the staircase to the main floor, Lord Amphetamine peered in each direction before heading over to the main entrance. Yet when seeing Valorian walking toward the doors, he halted his escape and quickly turned around, most certain he would be instantly recognized. Seeing a staircase to his right, Lord Amphetamine climbed up to the second floor, frustrated in knowing escape would prove more difficult now.

Recognizing where he now stood, Lord Amphetamine shuddered in fear, thinking of the purposes each room on this floor held. The citizenry of the white city had been grossly mislead in the belief that these rooms where places for re-education and re-indoctrination. In truth, the pure white walls of Remington House concealed nightmarish chambers of torture, profane experimentations, and gross neglect. Few held the mental fortitude to survive within. And for those who did, they were never the same after being allowed to rejoin society. Lord Amphetamine believed these citizens were to serve as a reminder to others that the elite and powerful were always watching and free will and the abandonment of conformity would under no circumstances be tolerated.

Wandering by each door, Lord Amphetamine braved glances into the room while feeling nauseated in recognizing the barbaric tools utilized by the sadistic physicians. Yet what disturbed him far more were subtle sounds resounding through the death-like quietness. Where these the echoes of ghosts forever interned with this hell or were they residual traces from past tortures? Hastening his pace, Lord Amphetamine silently prayed in not discovering the answer to this.

When approaching the last door on the left, a metallic sound much louder than other noises on this floor drew his attention. Swallowing hard, Lord Amphetamine found enough courage to peek inside the room. Startled by the presence of a young woman restrained by a straightjacket and sitting in a wheelchair, though darkly exotic in skin color, paleness in complexion complimented with the polished white walls and floors proved exactly how he thought ghosts might appeared when haunting the living. Her bewildered melancholy expression reflected the emotional torture he guessed she'd suffered.

Unexpectedly glancing toward him, with his eyes entranced with her, Lord Amphetamine now recognized the woman sitting in the chair. Etched deep in his memory, he recalled the striking lilt in her voice, the pleasant way her eyes blinked, and the shape of her lips. From the first moment they met at the educational academy, he had secretly fallen in love with her. Always smitten by her beauty, afflicted with severe shyness in his youth, he'd never found the courage to speak to her, his saving grace he thought. To express even one utterance of love was a punishable crime here in the white city. So he suffered miserably in silence, as all citizens did when conflicted with prohibited notions of desire.

Unthinkingly mumbling *"Marisol,"* under his breath, his heart lodged in his throat when she quickly looked at him, having been alerted to his presence.

"William?" she whispered. His heart nearly burst through his chest when hearing this. He had not heard his real name spoken to him since several years ago.

"That…is a name I once was known by…from a lifetime I have now forsaken. Yet, I cannot deny how long I have yearned for you to speak it." Slowly approaching her, he whispered, "This is no place for someone as sublime as you. You have only to ask…and I shall steal you away."

"Then I ask, no…I *beg*," Marisol responded, breathlessly.

"Are you able to walk?" Attempting to move her leg, the sound of the chain restraining her to the wheelchair echoed off the walls.

"A minor inconvenience," he mumbled, seeing her panic-stricken expression, trying to ease her fears. He noticed a white sheet on the examination table, sparking an idea. "You must remain still when I drape this sheet over you, not even *one* hint of movement. Feigning death will gain us access to the mortuary. I know of a passage there leading to a labyrinth of tunnels under the city."

Nodding her head, Marisol inhaled a deep breath as Lord Amphetamine covered her head and shoulders.

Wheeling Marisol down the hallway, Lord Amphetamine stopped when a nurse approached him.

"What is the meaning of this? Where are you taking this patient?" she insisted a response, causing him to timidly glance down.

"When delivering fresh sheets to the examination room, I found this patient dead in this wheelchair, ma'am. I thought best to remove the body to the mortuary before the next patient's evaluation."

"Splendid thinking on your part, *Arthur*," she commended him, referring to him by the name on his shirt tag. "Proceed."

"Yes, ma'am," he muttered, while bowing his head. Continuing down the hallway, he pushed the wheelchair into the lift and pressed the button for the mortuary level. Deeply exhaling his relief, Lord Amphetamine whispered, "Still with me, are you?"

"Yes," Marisol answered, faintly.

Breathing in air tainted by the strong scent of formaldehyde masking the stench of decaying flesh, they unfortunately drew the attention of the mortician when exiting the lift. "What do we have here? Once more they fail to notify me of another stiff being brought down," the mortician complained.

"I warned them you'd be displeased," Lord Amphetamine lied.

"Displeased, alright I am," the mortician barked back. "I have a mind to get on that lift and go up there to share with them my frustrations."

"I *would* if I were you," Lord Amphetamine encouraged him. "Why they just strut around up there, believing their superiority over us hard working gents."

"*Right you are!*" the mortician responded. Fueled with anger, he stormed over to the lift, closing the caged door when stepping in and pressing a button.

Waiting until the lift ascended out of sight, Lord Amphetamine quickly tugged the sheet off Marisol and started unfastening the restraints of her straightjacket.

"You may well have just sent that man to his...death," Marisol remarked but then clearly stunned when seeing the many dead bodies strewn about. "Oh...my," she uttered, under her breath.

"Too many disappearances have failed to go unnoticed by the citizenry here in the white city," Lord Amphetamine revealed, while freeing her from her restraints. "There is a heaviness weighting the air with anxious stares being passed from one to another as if they are in anticipation for something to happen. It feels like being on the edge of night and watching the horizon for that burst of daylight, only for this place...that daylight never comes."

Freeing her arms, he then found a pair of bolt cutters on the mortician's work table. Retrieving them, growing nauseous by how blood-encrusted they were, he carried them to Marisol's wheelchair. Kneeling in front of her, he struggled to break the chain.

"Hold...*still*," he muttered.

Seeing the chain snap, his chest heaved from labored breaths as he stood up. Assisting Marisol in standing, Lord Amphetamine led her by hand over to a manhole cover on the floor at the far end of the mortuary.

"Look for dim lights when you get down there. We must follow their path until finding one above a metal door," he urged, prying the cover open.

Trailing behind Marisol, she muffled a scream when seeing rats scampering about. Through what seemed like endless turns through the labyrinth, finally they arrived at the last light set above a partially opened metal door he spoke of. Passing by her, Lord Amphetamine led her to the bottom step of the clock tower.

"Now we climb," he said, while pointing up.

Both were nearly out of breath when reaching the clock mechanisms at the top. Slumping down against the wall, Lord Amphetamine closed his eyes and buried his face in his palms.

"William," he heard Marisol whisper. He spied out through his fingers, dragging them down to his chin when seeing her anxiously staring at him.

"From the first moment when I saw you, I was held spellbound," he admitted, looking at her. "I must confess that every hour in your presence proved blissful misery for me. I would find ways to be near you yet lacked all courage in speaking even one word to you. And when you would innocently look at me, my heart would be set afire. To feel such *elation* and *euphoria* over another's existence and be forbidden to express such emotions felt very much as a death sentence. Discouraged by this reality, in turn I became a skilled liar in denial of my desire for you. Over time, in further searching for relief to numb my tortured thoughts, I filched amphetamines from the hospital stores where I was employed as a custodian, an *honest* profession for someone as dim-witted as me. I sacrificed myself to the seduction of addiction, *desperate* to banish the throbbing of my broken heart."

"I never imagined you held such feelings for me," Marisol responded.

"My skill as a liar…thus proved flawless, one of few aspects of my life I found success with. Over time, my addiction drove me to carelessness and I found myself under arrest for my crimes. Rather than forced to endure re-education and re-indoctrination protocols, I, as well as three others, were banished out into the daylight on a derelict skyjammer the elite had come in possession of."

"Why was I not aware of this?"

"I know for certain I am not the only skilled liar in the white city. I imagine Valorian has much at his disposal enabling him to conceal anything his heart desires."

"How were you able to survive in the sunlight, completely impossible for us nightdwellers?"

"In this day and age, little is *impossible*," Lord Amphetamine offered. "For almost five years now, the elite have kept hidden the development of a serum curing our inability to withstand direct sunlight. The four of us were injected with this serum. I believe, however, our survival was not expected."

"Why would they keep such an astounding breakthrough hidden?" He smirked at her dismay.

"The citizenry would then be compelled in demanding inoculations with such serum…and then abandon the night. With no one left to act as their slave labor, who would the elite rule?"

"So, in fact, we *are* no more than prisoners," Marisol mumbled, staring vacantly away.

"Yes, that *is* our reality. In addition, were the citizens to demand access to this serum, how *would they* escape the night? Ponder this for a moment. Should a catastrophic event threaten and damage the white city, how would the citizenry be evacuated, and to where?"

"To my knowledge, no evacuation protocols exist."

"With each one of us perishing," Lord Amphetamine affirmed. "My dear, even the grand Titanic from centuries ago, held more promise for survival than this mastery of technology we orbit a dead planet on. We have *no* lifeboats, and no one would arrive in time, even if we did." He leaned back, resting his head against the wall.

"Why were you taken to Remington House? What crime were you charged with?"

"Violations of morality and sedition," Marisol answered, while ashamedly looking away.

"I find those charges difficult to fathom, being that you were once Valorian's protégé. If I may ask, what demon possessed you to pursue such non-conformity?"

"I succumbed to my attraction…to a daylighter," she confessed. "And, in doing so, I questioned the moral and social fabrics of our society thus in violation of sedition."

He sat up, stunned by hearing this.

"Was the name of said daylighter…Sage?"

"Yes. How do you know this?"

Emptying his pockets, he revealed having the sun medallion and handed it to her.

"I regret to say that Sage, along with three of my friends, all were exiled by Valorian to the Earth's surface to perish."

Unexpectedly lunging over to him, Marisol gripped his arms while speaking the impossible.

"Then we must save them."

Reeling with defeat, Lord Amphetamine slouched back while shaking his head.

"No means to do so are at our disposal."

"That is not true," Marisol frantically argued. "I know of one way, yet it will require a diversion of epic proportions…as well as a skilled pilot."

"Is there somewhere hidden within the white city…a *skyjammer*?" he asked, wide-eyed with wonder.

"Some might call it that," Marisol confirmed. "Another might think of it as a time machine."

Chapter Nine

Enveloped by the night sky while falling to Earth, Sage gazed not only at the expansive stars shimmering across the night sky but also a faint crest of first light corrupting the distant horizon. The return to his life in the sunlight was so close, yet now impossible. Believing he would soon be dead, he focused his eyes on that sliver representing the past he desperately wanted back.

Violent flashes of illumination bursting below, however, soon drew his attention away from that which he no longer could have. Seeing bolts of lightning shattering across the blackness, Sage wondered if he'd be electrocuted before reaching the ground. Even through his protective helmet he could hear the sounds of the wind velocity and resounding explosions of thunder.

Struggling to feel for the rip-cord of his parachute, having no experience with this he wondered when the proper time to yank on it would come. Failing to see the other three, Sage knew he wouldn't be able to follow their lead when watching their parachutes deploy.

Again drawn to the severity of the array of lightning, Sage noticed something else, brightness emanating through the dense cloud cover. This reminded him of old black-and-white photographs he'd studied when younger of ghosts haunting historic homes and buildings. His mom had told him that most people believed in the presence of spirits, with others rejecting evidence presented. If such spirits existed, he hoped he would see his parents down there waiting with open arms.

Noticing the billowing cloud cover much closer now, taking a deep breath of oxygen, Sage then yanked the rip cord, sending his body soaring high as the parachute unfurled. Spiraling out of control for a minute, he then began floating downward, feeling his body being pulled by gravity. Gripped by chilled air when first falling from New London, Sage now felt strange warmth while descending into the clouds. The brightness he'd earlier noticed seemed more intense. However, droplets of moisture pelted his goggles with continuous flashes of lightning momentarily blinding him.

Captured by an intense updraft, Sage swirled out of control through the clouds but then felt his body plummeting. Revealed by the unrelenting lightning, the ground drew closer and closer. From what he could see of below, a bleak landscape awaited his arrival. Sporadic, barren trees stood as sentinels amidst a decimated forest. Yet, while gazing out in the distance, his eyes enlarged when seeing the destroyed remnants of a city. Keeping his eye staring there, Sage was struck by how this city failed in comparison to ones he'd studied. What was left of this appeared to have been built on a platform having crashed into the ground. Protruding shards from a shattered dome confirmed the obvious, that at one time it had been a floating city much like New London.

Landing feet first on a hillside, Sage skidded down the petrified wooded slope until colliding with a large boulder, knocking him senseless down to the ground. Dazed from the impact, his vision was blurred as he looked around, attempting to focus. Winded and feeling throbbing pain radiating through his body, Sage winced when trying to move. Although nothing seemed broken, every part of his body ached.

Shuddering in fear when strongly grabbed from behind, the air rushed from his lungs until he realized he was being embraced by one of his friends. Stumbling back, he watched his friend remove his breathing mask and helmet, revealing Adrenaline's anxious expression underneath. Seeing him take a deep breath, although frowning, Adrenaline nodded in urging Sage to follow his lead. Unplugging his breathing tube, and pulling off his mask and helmet, Sage coughed when inhaling the heated overpowering reek of smoke and burned wood.

"Have you seen Heroin and Lithium?" Sage asked, following the reverberating sounds of thunder.

"*Stay...down,*" he heard Lithium's hushed voice urge before Adrenaline could respond. Struggling up the hillside, through a veiling mist they noticed shadowed movements. But as Sage took another step forward, someone dragged him back, forcing him to the ground. Seeing Heroin place her finger to her lips, her panic confused him, though he remained quiet. Glancing just beyond her, he noticed both Adrenaline and Lithium also pressed to the ground.

Hearing animal-like growling, Sage peeked up from their hiding place, seeing many shadowed figures wandering away. A moment later they appeared to converge on something.

"*Another fresh one, a soldier maybe,*" a deep voice rasped out. The following sounds reminded Sage of feeding frenzies, he remembered studying, of animals in the wild. The four lay there, for endless minutes, hearing shredding and tearing sounds intermixed with agitated snarls.

After a while, Sage noticed a quiet stillness return to the heated air. As none of the others seemed prepared to move, he looked up to the cloud cover, still seeing its ghostly glow and lightning bolts passing from cloud to cloud. Sage wondered what could cause such a phenomenon, knowing the sun would not be shining overhead. However, he felt relieved in having this false light beaming down, enabling them to view their surroundings.

"I think we should find shelter," Sage suggested. "I don't want to be caught out in the dark with those people wandering around."

"By sinking their teeth into human flesh, they have forsaken their claim to humanity," Lithium argued. "They are no more than animals now."

Taking hold of his hand, Heroin nodded her agreement in Sage helping her stand. But his pulse began racing when Lithium wandered toward where the people shrouded in the mist were.

"Where are you going?"

"I want to see who they were feasting on?" Lithium answered. "I believe we need to know."

Following him into the mist, they soon found human skeletal remains but, what disturbed Sage most was recognizing the remnants of a security guards uniform, one very familiar to him. And, when looking at the skull and seeing a hole in the temple, if wasn't hard to figure out how this man died.

"Was he—?"

"One of the security guards who captured us?" Adrenaline finished Heroin's question. "Yes, I am most sure of it." Her eyes enlarged by fear.

"So they—"

"Devoured him," Adrenaline completed her words once more.

"We must all tread with caution. Cannibals…may not be our only threat here," he continued.

"Agreed," Sage offered, while reassuringly tightening his grip on Heroin's hand. Resting her head against his shoulder, he wrapped his arm around her for further comfort. He glanced back up the clouds. "We should get moving. We don't know what's causing that glow or how long it will last. Do you think we should take our parachutes with us?"

"No," Lithium answered. "They may prove too cumbersome to carry over a long distance and would without doubt slow our progress."

"Which direction should we go?" Heroin asked, fretfully. "I see nothing but a dead world."

"Maybe we could find a hiding place somewhere over there?" Sage wondered, motioning toward the fallen city ruins.

"We should forage among the wreckage for things to use as weapons," Lithium urged. "I fear the other inhabitants of this decaying planet will not embrace our arrival with friendship. Neither will this world."

Pointing beyond the city, all watched in awe as white twisters further decimated the land. The funneling motions of cloud near them left Sage worried the clouds would spawn more. His studies of the destructive nature of tornados all the more convinced him the need to find shelter. Strong gusts of wind against their backs seemed to agree with Sage as their pace quickened.

"What of Lord Amphetamine? What will happen to him?" Heroin asked, bringing up something no one had spoken of.

"He will find means of survival," Adrenaline answered. "Fear not for his safety. Of all us, he is by far the most-versed in the artistry of survival. He will find a way."

With all falling silent again, Sage looked out at rolling shadows crossing the desolate landscape. To him it seemed as if something had for a moment blocked the above glow. Yet when glancing up, no traces of anything to cause this could be seen. Fixing his view on the ruins, patches of mist clinging to the charred ground lay between them and the city. The absence of sounds with exception of thunder and their boots grinding upon wood and stone felt unnerving. A thought to say something was quickly dismissed as the need for quiet prevailed. If there were there dangers lurking out of sight, Sage hoped to not draw their attention to him and the others.

Tiring from walking over uneven terrain, Sage thought to suggest they stop for a moment to rest. But it was Heroin who halted first when reaching down for something capturing her attention. Having seen a dirt-covered lifeless face protruding through the ash, into her hands she cradled a small dark-haired china doll wearing a soiled white lace dress.

"What is this?" she curiously asked. Sage half-smiled.

"It's a toy. Little girls used to play with things like this, at least that's what my mom said. She told me she had several when she was growing up. Didn't you ever have one?"

"No," she answered while thoughtfully trying to brush the ash and dirt off it. "What do you do with it?"

"Well, you use your imagination to play games with it. You pretend it's your best friend or child and have fun with it."

"But...why?" Heroin continued to ask, clearly having no idea behind the concepts of toys.

"It's just something kids pass the time with," Sage remarked. Remembering what Marisol said about how children grew up on New London, he guessed that playtime with toys and fostering children's imaginations wasn't part of their upbringing.

After reaching the crest of a knoll, all four stopped dead in their tracks when discovering the skeletal remains of many adults and what appeared to be children strewn about. Lacking any traces of flesh clinging to the bones, Sage wondered how long ago the carnage taking the lives of these people had occurred. Amidst the bones lay personal belongings and tattered and shredded remnants of clothing and shoes. Heartbreaking to see, a wheelchair and a baby carriage were also close by.

"What happened here?" Heroin mumbled, under her breath.

"I should think the answer would be obvious," Adrenaline commented.

"I see no traces of weapons used to defend themselves," Lithium confirmed, while meandering through the skeleton field. "It *is* possible they had none to begin with. Being in possession of personal weapons was forbidden on all the orbiting nightdweller cities. What weaponry did exist were under strict control of security forces. These wretched souls held no advantage to thwart an attack."

"Do you think the people we saw earlier were the ones who killed them?" Sage asked.

"Yes," Lithium responded, glancing away. "The evidence is undeniable. We should not linger here. With the wind pressing against our faces, they remain blind to us. Yet should the wind shift, it will carry out scent, drawing them to us."

Slowly stepping over to the baby carriage, Heroin leaned down, gently placing the doll next to it.

"I believe these two belong together," she said. Backing away, she took hold of Sage's hand while continuing in staring at the doll. Brushing strands of her windblown hair away from her face, Sage then eased her to him with her resting her head once more against his shoulder.

"Come on with you," Adrenaline urged, taking the lead with Lithium following. Moving away from the carriage, Sage and Heroin found their places behind them, neither looking back.

Chapter Ten

Intending to gain entry into a classified laboratory under the Cultural Ministry, before Marisol could expose her electronic security wristband to the wall sensor, Lord Amphetamine grabbed her arm.

"My dear, you are now considered a fugitive. By gaining access with your security clearance, the authorities would be alerted to your location. I pilfered this off an orderly at Remington House," he revealed, exposing a security wristband of his own. "With luck, we should hope his security clearance is broad in spectrum. Although, there is the concern that he has regained consciousness and by now has noticed it missing, a risk we must take."

Pressing his wristband to the sensor, after an excruciatingly long minute, the door opened. Stepping inside the cavernous laboratory, overhead lights quickly flashed on, revealing what appeared to be a repaired and fully, operational skyjammer.

"Technicians have been laboring to restore Sage's skyjammer, as well as making modifications to enable it to travel in the darkness…by directive of Governor Valorian," Marisol divulged.

"Was it his intention to release Sage?"

"Not to my knowledge," she responded, glancing away.

"Did you reveal the existence of this to Sage?"

"No," she answered, continuing to look away.

"Why?"

"I had hope in convincing him to embrace life here."

"I see." Briefly placing a finger to his lips, Lord Amphetamine continued. "Once more I am confronted with the knowledge that I am not the only skilled liar in the white city."

"Sage very much believed himself a prisoner and, as much as I attempted to dispute this, the truth he clearly understood was undeniable. He would never have been allowed to leave," she confessed.

"So you callously stood by, watching him suffer with the misery in knowing his freedom was lost forever, when his means for escape proved so very close?"

"I loved him," Marisol argued.

"No," Lord Amphetamine rejected this. "You fell as prey to the seduction of addiction. The daylighter became your obsession. When with him, you tasted the fruit of euphoric elation and when away from him the cravings you felt to be with him left you barely able to breathe and reason in rational thought. No, my dear, you did not love him. If you truly did, you would have set him free."

"That is what I am attempting to do now, should he and your friends have survived their fall to Earth," Marisol responded.

"An *attempt*...spoiled by failure," Governor Valorian remarked, startling them both when stepping out from behind the skyjammer along with several security guards.

"Hello, Father," Lord Amphetamine greeted, and smirked.

***

Wringing her hands in her lap, Marisol seemed anxious in looking on as Valorian silently paced before them. Lord Amphetamine understood the internal struggle reeling in her mind. The brilliant man she held in the highest esteem, one far beyond reproach, in truth was no more than a cunning liar and a sadistic tyrant. His intelligence had been corrupted by the seduction of power, an all-consuming addiction. When idols fall, those who worshiped them suffer emotional damage, leaving them broken and empty, a place she was now falling to.

Wincing in pain from the tightness of the restraints binding his arms to a chair, Lord Amphetamine wondered why Marisol had not been restrained. The security guards had barely touched her while forcing him to the ground. Thoughts of this vanished when his captor began speaking.

"I should have murdered you rather than banishing you from New London," Valorian addressed his son. "Your aptitude for survival when faced with imminent death is a trait I severely underestimated."

"Delighted to *surpass* my potential," Lord Amphetamine responded, bowing slightly.

"When the daylighter's derelict skyjammer was intercepted, after he was taken away to the hospital, hidden security cameras captured images of you and the others sneaking off. After that, it was only a matter of timing and setting the proper trap to rid our utopia of parasites such as you. When I apprehended the daylighter and your three companions in the clock tower, I knew at *that very moment* a scheme of unfathomable depth would be required in efforts to apprehend you as well. As it *so happens*, I found myself in the midst of an exceptional accomplice." Bowing to Marisol, Valorian offered praise. "My dear, no actress could have portrayed a role with such depth as you."

Locking eyes with Marisol, the clarity of her stunned expression revealed not an exceptional accomplice, but an unknowing one. With Valorian glancing away, Lord Amphetamine silently urged her to play along, believing Valorian might be teetering on madness. Though continuing in seeming distressed, Marisol nodded her head in understanding.

"I am...*honored*...by your faith in my ability," she remarked, cautiously.

Valorian beamed, hearing her response.

"Never were your intentions to assist me in doubt. Both in words and actions, the conviction you displayed in befriending the daylighter to the point of feigning romance and uttering seditious words, as well as luring William to the skyjammer, masked the depths of your loyalty to New London…and to me. Not for one moment could I entertain the notion that you would betray your reverence to our society."

"Yet you sought her arrest," Lord Amphetamine argued.

"*Regrettably,* those were the unfortunate actions of others, a misunderstanding I have since amended. Fear not, my dear Marisol. Doctor Leetchworth and Nurse Jasper shall never threaten you again…as they are no longer breathing."

"As for you, my son, I held hope to never lay eyes on you again. But, like a disease thought cured, at times the patient slips from remission such is my predicament. It is unimaginable that a highly valued, sperm donation from me could result in such a miscreant as you. I should have simply murdered you, as I have done with others and suffered no remorse."

"Fire away. I *am* unarmed," Lord Amphetamine challenged, while attempting to outstretch his hands. "Put an end to my unwanted existence."

"*Unfortunately*, I find myself compelled in declining such invitation. Now, more than ever, it is advantageous for you to remain alive."

"Enlighten me regarding this sudden change of disposition."

"I am dying," Valorian revealed. "Nonetheless, I may cheat death with his reaping. Both of my kidneys are failing. I have maintained by strength and health through dialysis. However, a time will come when this temporary solution will fail. You, my *son*, hold the key to my survival.

By having one of your kidneys harvested and transplanted into my body, I can go on living."

"You are barking mad in thinking I would willingly agree to make such a sacrifice."

"Believe me when I say that this choice is not being made lightly. I have conducted an extensive search through the lineage database for other more desirable potential donors, yet yielded not one suitable candidate. I had almost given up hope…until your unanticipated return."

"To my dying breath, I will fight to stop you," Lord Amphetamine rasped. "Not *one* life-sustaining organ of mine, not *one* ounce of my blood, will I ever agree to share with you."

"I believe your current circumstances should suggest to you how few, if any, options exist for your refusal. Rest assured, my *son*, once the surgical procedure has been successfully accomplished, no further harm will come to you. We are both relatively young and strong. However, in time I may require further physical sacrifices from you in efforts to maintain my longevity."

"You demented bastard," Lord Amphetamine mumbled, under his breath.

Revealing a syringe from his top desk drawer, Valorian began walking toward his son until stopped by Marisol.

"I believe I hold far more experience in the use of syringes," she remarked, nervously. "I know the exact point of entry the needle should pass through for optimum potency."

"Of course," Valorian said, appearing pleased Marisol would take the initiative to inject his son. "This is a sedative that hopefully will send him on to his worst nightmare."

Nodding her head when taking the syringe from him, before Valorian could react, Marisol stabbed him in the throat, sending him staggering back. With his eyes enlarged by shock, Valorian slumped down and within a minute lay unconscious.

***

Quickly unfastening Lord Amphetamine's restraints, Marisol was about to turn away when he pulled her to him for a passionate kiss.

"For too long...I have wanted to do that," he whispered.

Awkwardly stepping back, the way Marisol now saw him altered so much from only moments before. Conflicting notions flooded her mind when thinking of what to do next. With her pulse raging and butterflies surging in her stomach, taking a step toward him, she caressed his cheek and kissed him back, seeing his grin when their lips parted.

"Now what, lovely?" he whispered.

"You must pilot the skyjammer down to the Earth's surface to rescue Sage and your friends," she encouraged, regaining focus.

"Not without you."

"You *must!*" she insisted. "I will create a diversion which will enable you to steal away. It is a risk we must take if we are to save Sage and your friends. Trust me."

"I do." He kissed her a final time. "Say my name once more...so I may reclaim it from the lips of the woman I love."

"William," she responded, breathlessly.

He smiled.

"How, my lovely, do I get passed the guards on the other side of the door?"

"Bind his arms behind his back while I devise a plan for that," she answered, motioning toward Valorian.

Stepping over to Valorian's desk, Marisol understood the answer to this question lay amidst the private information she believed Valorian kept in his personal database. Yet gaining access would prove no small task. To obtain this information, she would need to know his numeric, four digit security code. Without this, and recognizing Valorian would never divulge such information, they were helpless.

Thinking of any, and all likely four digit codes, from well-known, historic dates to random configurations, none yielded success in gaining access. In frustration, she ran her hands through her hair before clenching her fists. Pondering the security code Valorian might use, she suspected this number would hold hidden meaning for only him.

Wandering over to the window, Marisol stared out at both the star-lit night sky and the white metropolis of New London. Sensing William easing behind her, she noticed both his and her reflected images on the dark glass. But when concentrating deeper on their reflections, Marisol spied the presence of another man reflecting back. Turning around, she studies an enlarged photograph hung on a nearby wall.

"Who is that man?" she asked.

"No idea," William replied.

"Identify," Marisol spoke, pulling out her personal communication device and snapping a picture of it.

"George Orwell," a synthetic, male voice responded.

"Elaborate," Marisol continued.

"George Orwell is the pen name for Eric Arthur Blair, born June 25, 1903, and living until January 21, 1950. A novelist, essayist, journalist, and critic, among his most notable publications are *Animal Farm* and *1984*. All works of George Orwell are banned in New London, having been deemed profane and seditious."

Marisol thought back to something Sage commented on with regards to George Orwell.

"*1984*," she had mumbled under her breath. Then returning to Valorian's computer, she typed the digits 1-9-8-4 and watched with her eyes enlarged while gaining access to his most private information.

"Success," William whispered, from behind her. "And now?"

"Truth," Marisol answered.

Chapter Eleven

Feeling drained and lightheaded and with the strong gusts of wind shifting, Sage knew they'd need to find shelter soon. As far as his eyes could see, other than the massive ruins of the once orbiting city still at least a mile ahead, the isolation clear in each direction offered few options. However, two structures, a dilapidated farmhouse and a severely damaged barn seemed a likely place to hold up in for a few hours. Yet out in the open, fully exposed to the harsh elements as well as lacking protection from the cannibals, he wasn't sure how safe this place would be.

Wisped by the relentless gusts, remnants of tall grass lining the dirt road they walked along appeared as if waving them to keep walking. Wandering closer toward the farmhouse, he watched a porch swing haunted by the breeze and saw a gate tapping against what was once a white picket fence. Stopping by the mailbox, he glanced up toward the sky, noticing how rapidly the cloud cover was passing and hearing rumbles of distant thunder. After looking again at the house, Sage turned to the others.

"Maybe we could stay here just to rest for a few hours."

"Yes, I believe we should," Lithium sighed, in agreement, though clearly reluctant. Both Heroin and Adrenaline nodded their approval as well.

Taking hold of Heroin's hand, Sage smiled slightly while leading her through the gate and up a weathered brick sidewalk to the front porch. Seeing a welcome mat greeting them at the front door, Sage couldn't help but grin wider. And when all had stepped on to the porch, Sage shrugged his shoulders and knocked, not expecting an answer. But when hearing "Who is it?" asked from inside, they all stumbled back off the porch. With the sounds of several locks being unbolted, Sage felt his pulse racing as the door finally opened. Appearing in the doorway was an older tall thin Japanese-looking man wearing a baseball cap and a Chicago Cubs jersey.

"Hello," he greeted them, cheerfully, his English unexpectedly spoken with an accent Sage wondered about.

"Aren't you worried we might hurt you?" Sage asked, surprised by the man's relaxed attitude.

"Why would I be?" the man answered, casually. "Y'all *knocked*. Those animals out there wouldn't have." Stepping out of the house, he adjusted the reading glasses on the bridge of his nose while staring at Sage. "I reckon I never thought I'd meet another daylighter."

"How do you know I'm a daylighter?"

"By the color of your skin and hair. These others look like they've been in the sun, too, but not like you," the man urged, battered by the wind's intensity. "Come in. It's too dangerous to stay out here." He held up his hand, as if to say "*Wait!*" while reaching for something just inside the door. Turning back to them, this time holding a strange machine in his hands, the man apologized. "Sorry, but I need to check something first."

"What, may I ask is that?" Heroin uttered.

"This is a Geiger counter, ma'am," the man answered. "It's an instrument used for measuring ionizing radiation." Pressing the on button, its clicking noises intensified when he held it up to them. "Y'all have been exposed to high levels of radiation but it *may*…just be on the clothes you're wearing. Take them off and leave them out here. There are some clothes left inside from the home's previous owner you could wear."

Silently agreeing among themselves to do so, soon all four shivered while standing there naked until ushered inside by the man. Kindly offering a blanket to Heroin, he point up the staircase.

"Ma'am, the room on the left was once a girl's. I'm sure she left something you could wear. As for you boys, check the closet in the room on the right."

"Do you want me to go in there with you?" Sage asked Heroin, as she stepped over to the closed door. She kissed his cheek.

"I adore your sense of chivalry, yet I will manage on my own."

Rummaging through the closet and dresser, Sage, Lithium and Adrenaline each found clothes to wear, though Adrenaline's were somewhat tight due to his massive muscular frame. The black and white flannel shirt and faded blue jeans Sage wore, however, fit well. Leaving the room, Sage grinned when seeing Heroin wearing a white lace dress and black boots.

"Thank you," she remarked, bowing with a curtsy to his unspoken compliment.

Following Lithium down the staircase, when reaching the bottom step they saw no traces of the man. Calling out, Sage then heard noise coming through a door under the staircase. Cautiously tip-toeing over to it, he saw flickering light beaming from down another staircase.

"Please lock the door behind you," the man requested.

Crowding on the bottom steps, the man motioned an invitation for them to sit with him. The small space, having no windows and brick walls was warmed by fire from an iron stove. Breathing in the scent of burning wood, Sage also smelled the more pleasant aroma of soup cooking in a pot.

"Dinner will be ready soon," the man said.

"I wish I had more to share, but unspoiled food is scarce," the man apologized, while pouring a full ladle of soup into small bowls. "The supplies I have here are from what I could salvage from the wreckage of New Columbia."

"No apology is necessary, kind sir. We are most thankful for your gracious hospitality," Heroin responded. "I believe introductions are in order." Heroin didn't use the names Sage referred them by. "My name is Evangeline." She pointed to her left. "This is Sage and Richard and Brendan."

"I'm Professor Hideki Nakamura, but you can call me Bob."

"A pleasure to meet you, *Bob*," she spoke, with a slight bow of her head.

"If I may ask, what occurred on New Columbia, leading to her falling from the sky," Lithium questioned.

"An act of terrorism," Bob revealed. "Six months ago, an explosion near our nuclear reactors damaged the orbiting capabilities. Hundreds were killed, with about a thousand more dying when New Columbia took a dive into the Earth's surface. Those of us who survived had to fight off what's still living down here on the surface, which is more animal than people. When someone turns to cannibalism to survive, they give up their right to be called human. What's roaming around out there, well…it's like they've gone through de-evolution, reverting back to more primitive behaviors. As for those who survived the crash of New Columbia, I reckon I might be one of the left. I'm not real sure, just a feeling I guess."

"We found roughly twenty skeletons not far from here," Sage confirmed.

"Damn," Bob mumbled under his breath. He appeared to struggle in speaking. "Did you find a baby carriage?"

"Yes," Sage answered.

"I knew it," Bob uttered, shaking his head. "I warned them not to leave but they wouldn't listen to me." Reaching out, Heroin soothingly covered Bob's hand with hers. "They had no way to defend themselves. Son-of-a-bitch," he mumbled.

"Why were they leaving? Where did they think they could go?" Sage asked.

"Only half way around the world," Bob answered, while taking off his baseball cap and rubbing his bald head. "Before New Columbia fell from the sky, rumors were being spread around the other cities about a civilized colony of lunar survivors living on New Zealand's south island. Somehow they manage to return to Earth on a few of them space shuttles. Our governor, along with the governors of the other orbiting cities, intended to find out...but one after another something happened to each city. By the way you three talk, I'm guessing you're from New London and that your city has fallen, too."

"While your assumption of us being from New London is accurate, New London, itself, remains in orbit. Its governor, a vile-hearted demon named *Valorian*, confessed in causing the destruction of the other orbiting cities," Lithium revealed. Bob closed his eyes, shaking his head and rubbing his chin.

"New Columbia encountered a damaged shuttle from New London roughly seven months ago," Bob confirmed. "I don't know all the details surrounding it, but a bomb could easily have been smuggled into our city from it. I'm not sure how it would have been planted near the nuclear reactors."

"Maybe it was robotic, something remotely controlled?" Sage guessed.

"But it doesn't explain *why*."

"Are you familiar with the term *megalomania*?" Lithium asked.

"A condition of mental illness resulting in delusional behavior," Bob correctly answered. "A person suffering with this believes her or she possesses great power and importance, thinking of themselves almost as if—."

"A God," Sage interrupted. "But in this case no more than a liar and murderer."

***

Awakened by someone moving, Sage opened his eyes, spying Bob slowly climbing the stairs. After hearing the door unlock and him closing it behind him, Sage shifted his body away from Heroin who lay next to him. Cautious in not wanting to awaken his friends, Sage followed Bob. Stepping out into the hallway, he found him standing in front of a large cracked picture window in the living room.

"What time is it?" Sage asked, wondering next to him.

"Half passed the end of the world," Bob answered, sarcastically, causing Sage to smile. "No matter what time of day it *could* be, it always seems like moments away from the edge of night."

"Any idea where we are?"

"Definitely not in Kansas, but nowhere near Oz."

"Where were you born?"

"Nagasaki, Japan, but my parents moved to Dallas, Texas after I was born."

"Why does it look like sunlight is trying to penetrate through the clouds?" Sage wondered, still seeing the strange radiating glow across the sky.

"That's residual effects from chemical warfare," Bob explained. "Suspended in the water vapor, making up the clouds, the residue of unleashed chemicals and toxins hold phosphorescent properties, making it look like blocked sunlight. Occasionally, the clouds actually *do* part for a minute of two. If it's daytime above, a bright shaft of sunlight will shine all the way down to the ground. I call these *messiah shafts* because it looks like God is sending his light down to Earth, leading the dead to Heaven."

Through heavy fog clinging to the ground, Sage's eyes grew large in watching the shadowed silhouettes of the cannibals walking down the dirt road, passing the house without stopping. Growing light-headed by how his pulse was racing, when trying to step back out of fear, Bob grabbed his arm.

"No," he mumbled, faintly. "Trust me, they'll hear you," Bob warned.

After staying quiet for a few minutes until the cannibals were gone, Sage found the courage to break their silence.

"We need to get back up there, back to New London. We have friends who are in danger."

"Well, you're only asking for the impossible," Bob remarked, dryly. He focused his eyes outside. "Any airplanes, shuttles, or skyjammers still on Earth were either destroyed or are now useless piles of junk. And, even if you did come across one that might still work, I reckon you wouldn't find any fuel for it."

Sighing while running his fingers across his bare chest, and remembering the sun medallion taken from him by the security guards, what seemed like random thoughts suddenly began falling into place, resembling a puzzle with all pieces now joining. Bob's *Wizard of Oz* remark collided with Sage's memory of watching that movie with his mom on their computer. Adding to this, he remembered the black and white photograph of his dad and uncles standing in a field near a hot air balloon. They whispered together about having an idea. Both he and Bob stood deathly still when another cannibal appeared in sight, touching the fence gate while staring at the house.

Chapter Twelve

With so many files appearing on Valorian's computer monitor, Marisol felt overwhelmed in wondering which one to review first. Later, after more than an hour of searching though the information, both she and William were horrified by the depths of his uncovered, vicious acts. A staggering number of people suffered through, or had been murdered by his totalitarian vision, as well as his delusions of grandeur. He called himself a God while pursuing his dark divinity over New London. In truth, he was the incarnation of an angel of death.

Emotionally drained from exposing his madness, Marisol intended to halt her search, having yielded a bounty of incriminating evidence to bring an end to his reign of terror. When seeing her own name attached to one of the files, her interest was sparked. The latest, security picture taken of her was followed with biographical and educational information. What followed *this* left her astonished and speechless. Hidden camera footage taken from within her dormitory room documented moments when she was alone. Mundane daily footage had been edited out leaving only those times when she was naked or getting dressed. To her it was perfectly clear, Valorian's voyeuristic perverse addiction for her.

Clearly angered by what he watched over her shoulder, William rushed over to Valorian, forcefully pulling him up and then slamming him against the wall.

"You revolting bastard," he cursed, with Valorian awake but mostly incoherent. "You will pay for your crimes." He released Valorian to slump down against the wall.

Returning to Marisol's side, William reached to delete the file but Marisol halted him.

"No, this…is evidence against him. Skeptics of his treachery will require indisputable proof, no matter the cost to my dignity."

"Look at the screen," William urged. "The evidence of his evil is *undeniable*. This *one* piece of his horrific behavior can be omitted. It would devastate me to see you suffer further from it devilry. I beg you, *please*…delete it."

Brushing aside her tears, Marisol nodded in agreement.

"I will," she urged, composing herself. "Time is running out for our friends. You must pilot the skyjammer down to the Earth's surface to find them. Our position has maintained over where the fell."

"But…what if they failed to survive the fall?" William struggled to say. He watched her access surveillance footage revealing the moment Valorian banished Sage and the others to the toxic Earth surface.

"The still images from Remington House clearly show each one wearing a parachute," Marisol assured William. "I believe, in my heart, they survived the fall." She typed on the keyboard frantically, linking to the skyjammer's helm computer. "I will program the skyjammer with the estimated range in position of where they may have landed."

"Come with me," William pleaded, suddenly.

"No," she responded, quietly. "The security force guarding the skyjammer must be diverted away. This can only be achieved from here. I must see this through. Valorian must be exposed for his committed crimes. Otherwise, more will suffer from his brutality. I beg you to understand this."

"I…do," William reluctantly agreed.

"Then go. The outside security guards have left their post. You must hurry as they may only be gone for a moment or two."

Tilting her face toward his, their lips bound for what she thought might be their last kiss. When looking into his hazel eyes, her fear of this clearly reflected back.

"I love you. I always have," he whispered, and then backed away. Just before leaving Valorian's office, William looked at her one last time, attempting a smile, one corrupted with sadness.

"He will die with the rest of them," Valorian mumbled, soon after William left. Unnerved by his remark, Marisol fought to ignore him. "His professed love for you will be his undoing."

"And your *expertise* with love renders you the authority on this subject," Marisol argued. Valorian's wicked cackle further disturbed her.

"Oh, my dear, I have never embraced the foul concept of love. For me, *obsession* has proven far too enticing to ignore. Time and again, throughout history, those afflicted by love's seduction have followed a road to ruin. No, *love* and I have never been companions. *Lust*, perhaps…as I am *human*."

"I have my doubts of that." Her response sparked an evil grin on his face. She refocused her thoughts when finding the footage she and Sage had witnessed of the daylighter genocide. "Which facet of your *obsession* drove you to annihilate an entire population?"

"My actions were born out of fear," Valorian revealed, his expression turning grim. "What your daylighter *friend* never knew was of an epidemic spreading like wildfire among the daylighters, the origin of which we never discovered. Many believed the daylighter population had escaped Earth, unscathed by the genetic aberrations us nightdwellers suffered, a tragic fallacy. Early symptoms of their mentally, debilitating disease included painful migraine headaches, manic episodes, depression, aggression, and hyperactivity. William's friend, Richard, suffers with this disease. His once addiction to lithium has slowed its progression yet eventually he will succumb to its full effects, a brain aneurysm which will claim his life. All the evidence is there at your disposal."

"You *lie*," Marisol uttered, in rejecting his revelation. "What Sage and I viewed were torture and genocide."

"What you and the daylighter witnessed was my well-edited act of revenge fueled by my jealous rage," Valorian confessed. "A number of the images were in fact accurate. We *did* euthanize the infected daylighter population to stem a greater epidemic from infecting our own society. I strove in being as humane as possible. I am not the monster you believe me to be."

"And what of the fates of the other nightdweller cities? It was by your directive in seeing to their destructions."

"We knew they were in contact with the daylighter population. We shared with each the information regarding the epidemic and were startled in finding out how widespread the disease was among the other cities. At first we sought to quarantine New London from the other cities, yet they violated our requests to maintain their distance. So to protect our city, I sought a permanent solution to the dilemma we faced. And one-by-one when in breach of our demands to stay away, I authorized the delivery and deployment of a small-scale weapon of mass destruction to be positioned at critical points near their nuclear reactors. Once a safe distance away from them had been achieved, I remotely detonated said weapons."

"Murdering thousands."

"While saving others," he countered. "Especially *your* daylighter, the last of his kind."

"So, Sage is not infected?"

"No, his test results returned negative for traces of the disease. In viewing his medical records, all can be confirmed."

"How did Richard contract the disease? Is it spread through physical contact?"

"Among the daylighters, it appears genetically selective regarding who it infects. Hindered by our inability to screen the potentially infected, we were faced with no option other than to consider them *all* infected, much like the citizens of the other nightdweller cities."

"And you barbarically slaughtered every man, woman, and child, some of whom were completely healthy?"

"Justifiable considering the risk," Valorian argued. "William's friend Richard, however, was infected by a serum developed by our scientists in hopes of allowing our citizenry the capacity to endure sunlight once more. From the harvested DNA of a dying daylighter New London rescued, when formulating this serum our scientists were blind to this disease. The serum was tested on soldiers dispatched in making contact with other daylighters. All but Richard have now died, some naturally with the rest terminated in efforts to control any spread of the epidemic, as well as silencing them from revealing the fates of captured daylighters."

Staying silent for a moment, a dreadful new thought forced its way into her mind.

"What of William and the other two? They were injected with the very same serum. Are they also infected?"

"Mysteriously, no. Again, this lends to the theory of the selectiveness of the disease and the genetics of potential victims."

Rising from the chair, Marisol wandered over to the windows, once more viewing her reflection on the dark glass. Knowing her whole world, everything she knew, teetered on the brink of collapse, the emotional toll of being confronted will Valorian's lies and crimes weighed heavily on her mind. She knew what needed to be done, but felt conflicted in understanding the repercussions.

"Is there anything you regret having done? Or do you simply lack the capacity for remorse?"

"Are you suggesting I atone for my sins? I fail to see how an admission of guilt from me will change history. But to answer your question, no, I hold no regrets over what has transpired. I sought to foster a society unblemished by the failings of past generations." He fell silent for a moment. "I must amend my statement as I *do* harbor only one regret. Of all the citizens of New London, only *one* truly threatened my authority without ever understanding the power she held, that being *you*. My dear Marisol, you were the one flaw in my armor. Your beauty, your intelligence and thirst for knowledge, your unflinching devotion, all posed a threat to me as you were the only one who could challenge my authority merely by your existence."

"You fear me?" she uttered, stunned by his revelation.

"No," Valorian answered. "I am obsessed with you, a weakness causing me to be careless and reckless when the lure of you grows too much to control. Had I the clarity of uncorrupted reasoning, I would not have mistakenly thought of you as my ally."

Returning to his desk, Marisol accessed surveillance footage near the skyjammer. Believing William would soon arrive, she returned her attention in merging all Valorian's secret files into one.

"I *wonder* what satisfaction you will gain when exposing my secrets to the citizens of New London. If I am correct, that is your goal? The result will prove disastrous, mark my words. Unleashing flawed, human will is a force uncontainable. The ensuing chaos and violence will decimate the fragile fabric of our society. Some loss of life regretfully may even occur and all as a result of your *human* yearning for vengeance. Once the smoke vanishes, and the dead are removed, the crime *you* will have unleashed will transcend all crimes of my own creation. How will you live with yourself?"

"In truth, I am the first casualty of said revolution," Marisol explained, as she completed her task. "Having only now found the strength to allow my heart to feel anything, I am sending the man I am falling in love with to certain death as he attempts an impossible rescue. Should society view me as a villain, so be it. Yet you will hold one distinction I never will."

"That being?"

Slowly running her fingers across the keyboard, for a second she hesitated pressing the enter button…and then did so, sending all of Valorian's secrets to every personal communication device in New London. "As this information disseminates from *your* computer terminal, *you*, Governor Valorian, will be the *first* villain exposed."

Chapter Thirteen

"*Keep...still*," Bob warned, under his breath. Nervously swallowing hard, Sage tried doing just that though he could feel his pulse racing. The cannibal continuously tapped the gate against the fence, acting like a small child with a new toy. His head shifted in each direction, as if fascinated by his surroundings. Filthy, oversized, torn clothes, resembling an army uniform, hung on his emaciated frame. His eyes appeared sunken and dark but clearly alert. What struck Sage most was that, though a cannibal feasting on human flesh, this man clearly displayed intelligence as if reasoning in his mind about the farm house.

An unexpected occurrence started the man, luring his attention away from the house. Piercing the seemingly endless cloud cover, one of Bob's mentioned *messiah shafts* lit one of the barren trees at the edge of the nearest field. Seeing the man bolt away toward it, he soon joined a number of other cannibals arriving at the tree. With all reaching their hands up, they acted as though they wanted the light to take them with it, rescue them from the carnage of this decaying planet. But the light offered freedom for none as it quickly disappeared.

"Have any of them ever come in here before?" Sage asked, closely watching the crowd of cannibals disperse.

"Only onto the porch to look through the shattered windows," Bob answered. "When I first found this place, I cleaned out all the rotting food and the dead body of an elderly woman. Now this place only smells like wood, dust, and dirt. They won't come in here unless they smell something that's died."

"Did any of the farm animals or birds or anything like that survive the war?"

"Only the cockroaches, and lots of them. They feast of human flesh just like the cannibals."

"When the last one was watching the house, didn't he seem almost intelligent?"

"You saw that too?" Bob paused. "Yeah, he may have some smarts left about him. I'd reckon it would be a mistake to think they all weren't smart to some degree. They're all desperate and, if they're smart, that makes them a whole hell-of-a-lot more dangerous to worry about."

Hearing the soft creaking of floorboards behind them, Sage expected to see Heroin standing in the doorway leading toward the back of the house. But when slightly turning, his heart wedged in his throat in seeing the cannibal from outside standing there watching them.

"I know," Bob murmured, wanting to say something to Bob, before he could force a word from his dry throat.

"I'm not a monster. I'm…just hungry. That's all I know anymore," the cannibal mumbled.

Lightly exhaling and swallowing hard, when further turning toward the man, Sage inhaled the pungent mixed stench of body odor and rotting meat. Now staring at him, fully lit by the cloud glow flooding in through a high window near his head, Sage couldn't tell the man's age by how he looked. Having thin hair and missing teeth, he could have been eighty years old or more, yet his voice sounded softly young and deep. His cheeks and forehead were scarred as if he'd been burned. And noticing the jittery manner his hands shook as his side and the way his weight shifted from one leg to the other, Sage wondered if the man might be scared of them.

"What's your name?" Sage asked, calmly, though he felt frightened inside.

"I...think...it might be...Harley, but...I'm not always...sure," the man stuttered.

"How old are you?"

"I...don't know."

"What happened to your face?"

"I...got burned...by the rain."

"Concentrated acid at times," Bob confirmed, quietly.

"I'm hungry," Harley whispered, stuttering. "I'm not...strong like the others. I only...get...what scraps are left. I...don't want...to be like...this...but...I can't stop."

"Where are you from?" Sage asked, hoping to lure Harley's thoughts from attacking and wanting to eat them.

"We...used to live on an army base...in Oklahoma," Harley answered, appearing confused in trying to remember. "But...we ran out of food and water. People started fighting...and some died. We...turned on each other...and we were still hungry...so...we ate what we could find." Glancing around, seeming disoriented, Harley then stared at them, his eyes wide with his expression desperate. "Will you kill me?"

Stunned by his request Sage swallowed hard while shaking his head. Seeing tears stream down Harley's dirty cheeks, he felt heartbroken for him.

"No."

"Why not?"

"You don't deserve to die, friend," Bob responded. "I reckon you never asked for any of this to happen. You're a victim, just like us."

"I don't want to eat you but I *do* want to," Harley confessed. "Maybe that *does* make me a monster."

"No," Bob corrected him. "It just makes you tired and confused."

Looking away for a moment, Harley seemed to understand what Bob had said. Slowly nodding his head in agreement, he then stepped back away from them but then stopped.

You can't stay here. The rest of them will find you," he warned.

"Maybe…you could lead them away from us," Sage suggested. "At least, give us a little time to escape."

"I don't…know," Harley answered, despondently. "I'm just…a dumb animal…to the rest of them."

"No, friend," Bob countered. "I think you're real smart. I think if you put your mind to it you could lead them away. Just by talking to you, we both know you could do it."

Remaining still but then again nodding his head in agreement, Harley stepped further back and then disappeared from sight.

"Don't let them pick up your scent," Harley urged, before they heard the back door close. Sage and Bob both exhaled with relief but stayed still for a minute until sure Harley was gone.

"We all need to get out of here *now*," Bob urged.

***

"What you're suggesting pretty much amounts to suicide," Bob remarked, as they walked along but then reluctantly agreed. "Although it may just be the only way to get back up there."

After awakening the others, with Bob's urging, Sage and his friends dressed in the uniforms they'd worn when parachuting down to the Earth's surface, telling them the uniforms would provide protection from acidic rainfall. Bob wore clothing he also said would be resistant to this diluted acid. All five then began the mile trek to the ruins of New Columbia.

The stench of decay clinging to the hot, stagnant air left Sage wanting to take a few breaths of air from his oxygen tank. But having less than half a tank left, he knew he'd need it when attempting to leave the surface. Covering his nose when the air grew too rancid, he stared up at the phosphorescent clouds and watches the barren branches of a few trees rattled by gusts of wind. A thought crossed his mind that even down here on the surface he couldn't escape the lies. All who lived in the sky believed the Earth to be nothing more than a dead wasteland. But life, all-be-it sparse and savage, still found a way to thrive in the most primitive terms.

Large pieces of debris littered both the road and adjacent fields, adding to the already existing destruction left from the war. The center of the country, particularly here in northeastern Colorado and neighboring Nebraska, had been pummeled by incendiary bombings meant to destroy crops. Knowing how close they were to where his dad grew up, a thought crossed Sage's mind in wanting to find this place but there was no time. The skepticism of his plan by his friend drew him away from this notion.

"A *balloon*, hot air perhaps, are you mad?" Adrenaline uttered, in disbelief. "And where would one locate such relic?" Adrenaline pointed up at the flashes of lightning passing through the cloud cover, "Should it even be remotely possible for one to obtain such a contraption, I fear eminent destruction when rising into the storm."

"I understand your concerns," Sage offered. "If there was another way, I would gladly choose it. Even if we could find a skyjammer or vintage airplane, we wouldn't have the fuel needed for it. By using a balloon, the force from extreme wind updrafts could lift us high and hopefully above the clouds. I know it sounds crazy but I would rather risk the chance in trying to get back up there over staying here to wait to die."

Exhaling his frustration, Adrenaline seemed lost in thought as if attempting to further his argument against Sage's plan. Running his hand across the stubble on his face, it was clear he had nothing else to say. Sage felt relieved when seeing him reluctantly nod his head, relinquishing his objections.

Feeling Heroin take hold of his hand, Sage breathed a little easier, seeing her smile at him. They had shared a passionate kiss before she'd fallen asleep in his arms. Having her here with him drove his decision to pursue escape in not wanting her to suffer amidst such destruction and desolation. With every moment spent with her, Sage knew he was falling in love.

Another concern for Sage was Lithium. He'd awakened suffering a severe migraine headache. Stumbling a few times, Adrenaline made sure to stay close to Lithium as they continued on. Exchanging a concerned glance with Adrenaline, Sage noticed something in his expression, suggesting he knew something he might share with him later.

"So, you're sure we can find a balloon there?" Sage asked, turning his attention back to the road ahead and the massive ruins.

"Yes," Bob answered. "Meteorologists at the science institute used to launch them into the atmosphere for collecting data. The institute only suffered some structural damage when the city fell. A lot of the equipment was destroyed or damaged, but there may still be one or two weather balloons in storage. We should be able to find what we need. I still think its suicide…but I'm with you. I too reckon I'd rather die trying to escape instead of waiting down here to die."

Maneuvering through several large piles of concrete, all came to a sudden halt when seeing a swarm of cockroaches scavenging over decaying human remains. Covering their mouths and noses from the nauseating stench of rotting flesh, they quickly moved on. After walking just beyond this, Sage realized something.

"We need to get away from here *now*," he urged the others.

"He's right," Bob agreed. "The wind is going to carry that stench to the cannibals. Harley may not be able to keep them away from us when they smell that."

Bellowing calls sounding out through the mist to their right startled them. Panicked by this, Sage froze, fighting to breathe while panting for air. Dragged away by his arm, though dazed with fear, his senses soon returned when reaching a large pile of concrete to hide behind. Crouching low, all five huddled together as the frenzied voices of the cannibals grew louder. Deep guttural growling and aggressive snarls echoed out. To Sage, it was clear that the pack was feasting on the human remains. The sounds of a scuffle and cries of agonizing pain corrupted the rebounding noises. And as the feast continued, Sage felt nauseous, wanting to vomit but holding it in even as the roaring commotion intensified.

After what seemed an eternity, the sounds of the carnage eased and then ceased. Though frightened to move, Sage swallowed hard and then stood, turning to face Harley, standing there staring at him. Startled by this, what he saw behind Harley forced the breath from his lungs. Kneeling on his hands and knees, another cannibal, short and emaciated like Harley, was using his tongue in lapping up blood staining the ground. Acting as a dog would, the cannibal continued in the spirit of this by howling when noticing Sage. Gripped by fear, they all held still and watched as Harley slowly reached down for a large piece of concrete. Back stepping without so much as a glance down, Harley smashed the concrete against the other cannibal's skull while continuing to look at Sage. Raising his hand to wave, Harley's expression held no fear, just peaceful relief. Dragged back by Adrenaline, Sage nodded his head in understanding to their savior.

Bolting away, the five made it to the edge of the main ruins and once more hid when the cannibal horde converged on Harley. Seeing what appeared as the leader of the pack reprimanding Harley with the other standing around, Sage's heart nearly burst through his chest when watching him lift Harley harshly and hurl him through the air with him landing hard against the ground. Lying still, he appeared unconscious. And with the pack crowding around, Sage closed his eyes, knowing what was to come next. When sneaking further away with the others, hearing the bellowing of the pack leader, Sage's heart broke, praying Harley wouldn't feel a thing with his suffering coming to an end.

Chapter Fourteen

Seeing the security guards distracted in reading posts received on their personal communication devices, William easily snuck into the landing bay, hiding behind a massive battery generator. Peeking out from its edge, the guards clearly appeared angry while talking in hushed voices. Believing Marisol had achieved success in releasing Valorian's classified files to the citizens, he breathed a sigh of relief when watching the guards abandoning their post. Left alone in the landing bay, William quietly moved over to the interior entrance to close and lock the door, hindering anyone from entering before he could leave.

Surveying the skyjammer, all outer damage from the solar storm had been repaired. Noticing a few modifications, such as the addition of jet propulsion components linked to batteries charged by added wind turbines, she looked ready for departure.

Climbing in through a bottom hatch, from back to front William observed the repairs on the inside. State of the art technology updating both the battery cells and water vapor and filtration systems had been installed. Passing through the greenhouse, abundant fruit and vegetable plants seemed ready for harvesting to eat. The furnishing in both bedrooms and fixtures in the kitchen and bathroom had also been replaced. Even clothing and a laptop computer were provided along with an abundance of other supplies.

Climbing up to the helm, William noticed all components having been updated with the latest technology. The shortwave radio remained along with newly installed, satellite navigational and communication systems. Impressed by the scope of the repairs and upgrades, William needed only to open the landing bay's massive clear doors before setting out to rescue his friends. Communicating through an uplink to the automated control panel for the door, he successfully sent a command for the bay doors to open and watched as they slowly did.

Typing in departure commands on the helm, the skyjammer lifted off like a feather, hovering for a moment before drifting out of the landing bay. Once outside, having no need to deploy the solar sails, he engaged the jet propulsion systems to smoothly propel the skyjammer forward.

Though all appeared to be going as planned, a sense of dread enveloped him as he watched the pristine vision of the white city seeming smaller and smaller in the distance when gliding away. William also searched the stars, desperate to see one piercing heaven for the reaping of his wish. Should he ever return, he hoped to walk the streets as a free man rather than embrace his former brotherhood with the rats in the dark labyrinth buried beneath the metropolis. Regardless of either fate, he feared both without Marisol.

Casting thoughts of return aside, William concentrated on the task set before him, in truth an impossibility. A billowing screen of luminous clouds appearing like smoke rising from raging infernos shielded the Earth's surface. The violent array of lightning passing from one cloud to another left him fearful the skyjammer would be struck. If so, a power surge potentially could disable the navigational system and overload the solar batteries and jet propulsion components. And should this occur the skyjammer would be rendered powerless and plummet from the sky.

Studying the funneling motions of two clouds, he knew the severe updrafts of their spawned vortexes were scarring the landscape. Having studied weather phenomena at the educational academy, the destructive nature of vortexes and cyclones left nothing standing in their paths, causing him further anxiety for the safety of his friends.

Knowing the need to steer clear of these storms, William strayed off course in searching for less intense cloud cover to penetrate. Yet seeing an endless vista of explosive lightning stretching to the far horizon, he sighed with frustration, believing he'd find no breaks in the clouds or any traces of the tempest lessening with intensity.

***

Closing Valorian's office door behind her, Marisol hoped to steal away unseen. Yet the clamoring chaos of angry voices sounding out from the parliament building's first floor offered her first indication in the commencement of the revolution she'd set off in revealing the treachery of the elite. The day of reckoning had arrived for those in power, fueled by a generation now unleashing their rage against those who sought to control all aspects of their lives. Although curious to watch dystopia's end, for now Marisol's only desire was to hide for a while.

Walking away from the main staircase, when passing the partially open doors leading into the governing chamber, an eerie silence from within confused her. Expecting the voices of the elite council to be panicked and shrill, with no utterances sounding out her curiosity of their calmness led her to peer inside. Awe-struck by what she saw, Marisol stepped further in, finding the ruling council to be no more than projected holographic figures stilled as if their program had been paused. So many times she had viewed vibrant, life-like images of this council addressing the citizenry. Not even for a moment could she have ever been convinced she was viewing false appearances. Nevertheless, once more confronted by Sage's theory of New London existing as an elaborate lie, she regretted how blindly she'd embraced conformity by those flawlessly disguising the truth.

Hearing Valorian's office door being broken open by the agitated mob, Marisol snuck away from the governing chamber, descending a narrow staircase at the far end of the hallway. When reaching the bottom step, distressed voices arguing amongst themselves drew her attention to a small room near the building's rear exit. Peeking in, Marisol found two young women cowering in a corner. Both were dressed in black-revealing costumes that would have been viewed as vulgar and profane if worn in proper society. Dark exotic cosmetics had been used to paint their faces, another violation of appropriate style regulations.

"Please...release us," the taller of the two begged, when noticing Marisol. Seeing both chained to the wall, Marisol's stomach turned, believing both had been victims of Valorian's vile yearnings. Spotting the key next to an almost empty contraband bottle of wine and a crystal goblet on a table just out of their reach, Marisol retrieved it and freed the women, both of whom sobbingly embraced her before rushing away. Glancing around, feeling nauseated and flushed by obscene objects littering the room, Marisol staggered out to the hallway. At first, intending to close the door, instead she left it open, hoping the mob would discover this evidence of depravity. Every lie and act of evil must be uncovered, she thought.

Emerging from the back entrance, in viewing the city before her, its aura of unflinching conformity had perished amidst smoke and violence. Remington House, set opposite parliament across a city garden, was on fire. Billowing black smoke seeping through every window veiled the street with a grey pungent mist. Many of the inmates stood outside watching and cheering the blaze as outraged citizens had arrested the physicians and staff, all rounded up and being led away in chains and shackles.

Watching those citizens simply standing by in not partaking with the uprising, none-the-less Marisol noticed their silent revolution. From one to another, changes in the carriage and demeanor shone like rays of sunlight piercing the darkness. The intermingling of men and women, some holding hands with smiles abundant and with one couple openly kissing, their revolt consisted in unleashing love, a force she now fully realized as being uncontainable. Feeling lightheadedness and with butterflies surging in her stomach, Marisol, herself, truly smiled. She was not simply a bystander watching the birth of a brave new world. She also savored this glorious sensation. To her, a notion filled her thoughts that they were all teetering on the edge of night with dawn rapidly approaching. And even though they could not experience the direct sensation of actual sunlight caressing their skin, nothing could stop its invisible rays from penetrating to their hearts.

Reminded that revolution is a double-edged sword, her attention was drawn to Valorian being dragged out to the garden's center. There he was chained to a large white marble statue of an angel. Seeing the citizenry crowding near in a circle surrounding him, Marisol eased through those gathered until finding a spot near the front. Though some may have hoped that after being pummeled to the ground Valorian would beg for mercy, Marisol understood how false this expectation would be. Smearing blood away from his mouth, Valorian stood up in defiance to stare at the citizens. His tone offered no quivering trace of fear as he addressed all.

"I must offer my congratulations for each of you embracing savagery in your thirst for social annihilation. Your blatant contempt for both the political and moral standards your government sought to instill within you will lead to the disintegration of proper behavioral standards. Vice and corruption with now assume their places of authority with impending damnation so willingly embraced."

A man Marisol recognized from being held in Remington House, the one who had confessed his love for a woman, stepped forward.

"Your reign of terror and brutality ends now," the man pronounced. "The lies you have woven to seduce us all with conformity in creating your totalitarian kingdom now unravel before your eyes…yet you admonish us, the victims, in yearning for lives driven by love and passion and civility. For too long you have manipulated the truth in seeking your stay of power, one far more corrupt and vile than you suggest our freedom will unleash. I, for one, will no longer bow to you. I, for one, will no longer deny the desires of my heart. I, for one, intend to forge a new life in a world free of your tyranny."

Erupting with insane laughter, tears streamed down Valorian's face until regaining his composure.

"Strike me down if you will," Valorian warned. "Another will take my place, one seeking the same power I wielded."

"You and your council of devils will stain New London no longer," the man responded. "We have yet to apprehend the others…but there are few places to hide. No one will shelter such demons."

"Allow me to assist you in your search," Valorian offered. "Below parliament you will discover a labyrinth of tunnels, wherein a crypt holding their decaying remains will be found. Please pay them my most sincere respects."

"How did they meet their deaths," the man asked, though still somewhat bewildered.

"Cyanide poisoning, you see…*power*…is an addiction unlike others. Driven by jealousy and greed, it…does not like to share. Each of them desired to curb my authority, an unforgivable crime in my eyes. Therefore, I sentenced the twelve to death. As with *all* kingdoms, there can be only *one* ruler."

Glancing at those surrounding, the man yell, "Then bring forth the king's crown!" the man yelled, glancing around to those surrounding him.

Bursts of cheering from those gather grew louder when another man handed the skull spike apparatus once used by physicians in Remington House to the man. Raising it, he condemned Valorian to wearing it.

"I crown thee…King Valorian the Terrible!" he called out. Placing it on Valorian's bald head, the man stepped back to admire what he'd done.

"I am *no*…king. I am a God, one who shall reap vengeance upon those who have sought my demise. The hour of your celebration is at hand." He then vigorously began bashing his skull against the marble statue, breaking off a large piece which fell to the ground. As he continued, blood from the spike puncturing his flesh sprayed out, causing gasps from those watching. With one final thrust of his head back, the rear spike penetrated deep into his brain. Valorian's body convulsed for a moment before falling limp. Slouching to the ground, his dead eyes stared out at those who persecuted him. Stilled and silent, one by one the gathered citizens turned away, leaving Valorian's body bound to the statue but carrying with them visions of his suicidal end.

Only Marisol remained. Wandering close, she stared for the longest time at him. Conflicted with thoughts of hatred for the man she once revered, his notion of being a god proved a convincing lie he told to himself. In truth, he was a flawed man afflicted with the same human failings he sought to eradicate, as well as a victim seduced by power, his ultimate addiction.

Chapter Fifteen

When first seeing the wreckage of New Columbia from a distance, Sage was reminded of scenes from old science fiction movies he'd watched, showing spacecraft that had crash landed onto alien worlds. In truth, that's exactly what the nightdweller orbiting city was. All who had escaped war and desolation in seeking refuge in the sky had relinquished their rights to call the Earth's surface home. For generations scientist had searched for alien lifeform, never anticipating they'd only need to look at their own reflections in finding this extra-terrestrial race.

Now as they began climbing up through the inclining ruins, New Columbia appeared less an alien spacecraft and more the remnants of an ancient sloped city destroyed in a cataclysm. Not one structure survived intact from when the city had fallen. While maneuvering around massive shards of debris, Sage wonder what this place looked like before Valorian saw to its destruction. None of the architecture even remotely resembled any of the buildings on New London. And what of the people who lived here? Was their society free and thriving or were they also captives in an orbiting metropolis?

Seeing Lithium slouch down in exhaustion against a wall, all stopped for a brief rest. "How are you feeling?" Sage asked, easing down next to him.

"I believe my brain wishes to explode through my skull," Lithium responded, clenching his eyes closed from the pain he suffered.

"I've seen this before," Bob recalled. "We called it *Night Syndrome*." I know you weren't originally a daylighter but somehow you found a way to endure direct sunlight. Anyway, we'd rescued a family of daylighters.

Within days each one fell sick with the *same* symptoms, fatigue and migraine headaches being the first signs."

"*Please*," Lithium interrupted, begging, "I do not wish for my friends to know how this progresses. Already it is a burden for Adrenaline to endure. I can never keep anything from him," he finished, attempting a smile to Adrenaline, who looked on with concern.

"Is it fatal?" Sage asked. "I need to know."

"*Yes*," Lithium answered under his breath.

"*No*, not in every case," Bob corrected him.

"I fail to understand," Lithium responded, appearing stunned. "Our scientists and physicians came to the conclusion that all would die from this condition and that it would spread as an epidemic."

"Of the five survivors we'd rescued, three *did* die," Bob confirmed. "*However* the other two only suffered with minor symptoms which cleared up when treated with synthetic sunlight therapy. Also, none of us nightdwellers were infected. I reckon this *syndrome* or *disease* will either cure itself or slip into remission when you are exposed to direct sunlight."

Bursting to tears, Lithium covered his face as his body shuddered. Crawling over to him, Adrenaline held him in his arms, attempting to comfort his friend. With his voice quivering in anguish, Lithium mumbled through his sobbing, "*So...some of those people...that...devil Valorian...order to be...put to death...could have...survived?*"

"I reckon so," Bob answered, causing Lithium's sobbing to intensity.

Resting his head back, Sage blankly stared away, thinking of the images of daylighters being killed in the film he and Marisol had been forced to watch. Heaviness gripped his chest with his stomach in knots and his pulse racing. Never before had he thought of killing anyone. But if given the chance, he would gladly put an end to

Valorian's cruelty. Maybe then the citizens of New London would know what freedom feels like. Reaching over, Sage grasped Lithium's hand, hoping this gesture might convey that he didn't hold Lithium responsible for what happened to all those daylighters. Like them, Lithium was a victim but, unlike them, his friend carried with him the torturous burden of continuously reliving this nightmare.

"We need to get going. The science center is just beyond the ruins of those three buildings. If we hurry, we'll get there before the storm hits," Bob urged, hearing the echo of rolling thunder before seeing flashes of lightning.

With Adrenaline's help, Sage tugged Lithium to his feet. Embracing him, Sage noticed traces of relief though his friend's distressed expression.

"Come on," Sage said to him. "Let's find our way home." Seeing Lithium nod his head, Sage turned to Heroin, whose beautiful smile radiated to him. Together, they continued climbing to where they hoped to find the means for escape.

Assaulted by the intensity of the gusting winds, Sage and the other balanced as best they could while pressing on to the science center. Barriers of concrete and steel beams protruding through what were once walkways hindered their progress with the storm bearing down on them. Striking lightning and deafening thunder frayed Sage's nerves as every step proved treacherous.

Relieved when finally seeing the partially blocked doorway they needed to pass through, though hopeful they'd find the weather balloons undamaged, doubts about how to use them clouded his faith with his impossible plan for escape. Further complicating his thoughts, Sage also wondered what would happen should they succeed in rising above the clouds. *Would New London be near enough to float to? Would Valorian be waiting there to stop their return? And what if New London was nowhere in sight? What then?* Hearing the other's breathing hard, Sage wondered if they were gripped by the same fears reeling in his mind. Feeling lightheaded and anxious, with each step taken he felt his heart wedged in his throat and an ache in his stomach.

Reaching the doorway, Bob climbed through first. Being familiar with the science center, he would act as their guide in finding the balloons. Sage helped Heroin climb through next, followed by Lithium and Adrenaline. Once inside, the building itself appeared as if it had suffered the direct impact from an explosion. Everything in sight lay in ruin. And worse, among the debris were the decaying bodies of the dead, both men and women. Covering their noses from the rotting stench, they tread by these final resting places as Bob motioned for them to follow him up the severely bent remains of a metal staircase.

For a moment, worried the tilted structure would break way from its base, Sage fought to refocus his thoughts on the balloons and how to make his plan work. Hearing the grinding of disintegrating concrete and shattered glass under his feet, he kept his eyes on the others as his pulse raced and his chest heaved. Vibrations from the outside thunder shook the staircase, causing a cloud of dust to veil the air. He wished someone would say something to distract him from his fear, yet no one uttered a word

"I've reached the door to the weather lab," Bob called out.

Sage hurried his steps in catching up to the others.

Jammed in its frame, at first the door refused to budge even an inch in letting them inside. But after a few shift kicks from Adrenaline, it banged open. Stumbling through, Bob then helped the others slip through the doorway. As with all else he'd seen, every piece of lab equipment had been damaged. Several of the computer terminals were blackened and melted, possibly having caught fire from sparks. A burnt aroma hung in the air, suggesting this to be true. Seeing several tanks of helium, none seeming damaged, Sage's pulse raced even more in now thinking his impossible plan might actually work.

"Where would they have kept the balloons?" he asked.

"Over there, just inside the storage room," Bob answered, pointing toward another mangled metal door.

"Y'all need to clear all this stuff out of here except for the helium tanks. Sage, you come in here with me. I'll need help dragging the balloon out," Bob urged them.

Following his instructions, the other three began clearing the debris while Sage cautiously followed him into the storage room as the tile floor was slippery to cross.

Managing to crawl through the doorway, a smile burst across Sage's face in relief of seeing a large deflated weather balloon against the wall.

"It looks like there's only one here. Do you think it will be big enough for us to use?" Sage asked, excitedly. But he felt tense when Bob pulled him out of view of the others without answering his question.

"Listen to me. We don't have much time. I lied. I had to do it," Bob confessed, in a low voice, looking at Sage after glancing over his shoulder.

"What did you lie about?"

"You friend, Richard, I'm sorry but he's…going to die."

"What do you mean? You said—"

"I *said* that two of the daylighters survived *Night Syndrome.* They *didn't.* I heard Richard and Brendan talking when they thought everyone was asleep. Richard thought he was dying…and wasn't going to leave with the rest of you. I lied so that he would. No one deserves to die here. I hope you understand."

"Thank you," Sage responded, nodding his head. His heart felt heavy as he fought the urge to cry. Bob pointed, forcing his thoughts away from sadness.

"We have enough helium to fully inflate this. Considering the force of the wind outside, it should be large enough to lift all of us into the air. I'll pull it through the door while you push from behind."

"Wait!" Sage said, shaking his head. "How is this even going to work? Maybe we're just kidding ourselves."

Stepping over to him, Bob looked him in the eye.

"Listen to me. I understand your doubts. To be honest, I don't know if this will work. There's only one balloon, so we just got one shot at this. This *is* a large balloon and we've got a lot of helium to inflate it with. We'll figure out some sort of harnesses we can use to hold on to it. Once we have this all figured out, we'll drag everything outside and with luck the balloon will be captured by the wind and off we go to Oz."

"But what happens if we get up there and New London is gone?"

"I'd rather hitch a ride on a big, pink balloon into the night sky than become some feast at a redneck cannibal buffet. I reckon I'll never be able to feel the sun again, but I'll be dammed to give up even the slightest chance to see the moon. Now you just forget those doubts and help me get Dorothy, the tin man and the cowardly lion back up to the emerald city."

"It's actually white."

"And I actually don't give a shit what color it is as long as it's there."

"Hey, wait a minute," Sage uttered. "Does that make me the scarecrow?"

"Could be worse. You could be Toto," Bob answered, with a smile.

Dragging the heavy balloon over to the doorway, Sage watched Bob climb through and then felt him pulling. Pushing with all his strength, the balloon moved with little resistance.

"One more push should do it," Bob called out. With one final thrust, the balloon passed through the doorway but quickly disappeared. Hearing Heroin scream, Sage rushed to the doorway and looked into the lab, seeing her face buried against Lithium's chest and Adrenaline standing next to them, his eyes wide and his jaw dropped.

Looking away from them, the air rushed from Sage's lungs with his heart sinking in his chest. Somehow Bob slipped on the tile floor and had fallen against the wall. Impaled through his stomach by a metal rod spiking out from the cracked plaster, a large red blood stain seemed to be growing bigger. Bob's eyes frantically shifted about, clearly shocked by what had happened. Skidding down to him, Sage cradled Bob's face in his palms

"It's going to be alright. It's not that bad," Sage whispered, knowing he wasn't convincing anyone.

"Don't you lie...to me. Don't...you do...that," Bob demanded, choking with blood seeping from the edge of his mouth. Wanting to respond but, before he could. Bob reached out, touching Sage's head. "I'm sorry." He looked at the balloon. The metal rod had punctured it, leaving a gaping tear.

"It...will be okay," Sage mumbled. "We'll find another way."

"You...better. Don't y'all stay here...or I...swear...I will haunt you."

"I promise."

"Don't...let those...bastards...get to me."

"I won't," Sage whispered, fighting back his tears.

Seeing Bob nod and take his final few breaths, Sage caressed his cheek until his last exhale. Then closing Bob's eyes, reeling with sadness, all Sage wanted to do was cry. So he did.

Chapter Sixteen

Watching the temperature gauge rising, William grew anxious by how the clouds covering the surface were radiating heat. His worries over the scorching air his friends might be breathing in caused him more panic as a searched for a calm point in the storm absent of the furious array of lightning surging from one cloud to another. Plaguing thoughts that his friends may already be dead corrupted his focus. But not once did he think of abandoning his efforts to find them. His resolve not to fail guided him onward.

Also, conflicting his thoughts were his concerns for Marisol's safety. If her plan had succeeded in releasing all of Valorian's hidden files to New London's citizenry, he believed the city would be gripped by a violent upheaval, resulting in countless deaths. And after the elite were driven from power, then what? The political vacuum created in the aftermath of this revolt could potentially spawn further chaos. Would the citizenry, so unfamiliar with the concepts of freedom and democracy, struggle in creating a new order?

Tracking funneling cloud movements off the starboard side, his jaw dropped when seeing an unexpected break in the storm. Realizing this might be his only chance to penetrate the endless cyclonic barrier, he readjusted his course. Increasing the speed, he piloted the skyjammer to that point and held his breath as he began his descent. Feeling the intensifying wind velocity rattling the helm, William's eyes grew large while astounded by the strange luminosity of the veiling mist he traveled through. The blackness of night he'd left behind had been replaced with an unimaginable glowing eeriness soon revealing the surface's desolate landscape. Each direction viewed shone devastation as far as the eye could see, causing him to ponder how the wrath of men truly had seen to the demise of a once magnificent planet.

Further illuminated by explosions of lightning, William wondered how anyone could survive in such a harsh and unforgiving environment. Noticing distant twisters scarring the barren horizon while spotting no places to find refuge, his heart sank as he imagined his friends being confronted by such an impossible place. Yet he knew how strong of spirit Adrenaline possessed. If Adrenaline had survived the fall to the surface, he would make certain to his dying breath to protect the others. William smiled when thinking this, feeling reassured of his friend's determination to live.

Confirming the coordinates Marisol had programmed in estimating where his friends may have landed, William adjusted his course, regretfully in the direction of the distant twisters. Employing a searchlight in viewing the ground, a forest of scorched fallen trees and fields reminding him of a lifeless wasteland caused his heart to sink further. Not one structure appeared in sight. Matching the latitude and longitude to a map shown on the helm computer, this part of northeastern Colorado had been sparsely populated before the war, yet searching it now left William wondering if anyone had ever called this place home.

A sudden burst of white, revealed by the searchlight, corrupted the ashen covered ground. Erupting with nervous laughter, William's discovery of two or possibly more discarded parachutes resurrected his spirits. Now certain his friends had survived their descent to Earth, he thought for a moment of which direction they might have sought refuge. To the east lay the ravaged wasteland. Higher ground lay to the west, offering possible shelter amidst the more rugged terrain.

Veering the skyjammer west, away from the twisters, William's jaw again dropped when brilliant flashes of lightning revealed the dark silhouette of a city much like New London. Surging the skyjammer's speed forward, when gliding closer, he knew immediately that this was once an orbiting metropolis having fallen from the sky. The ruins held many similarities to New London, causing him to speculate which of the nightdweller cities this was. Rampant thoughts flooded his mind in hoping there may have been survivors and that his friends had sought refuge among them.

Easing back the speed of the skyjammer, William initiated a hovering device near the edge of the ruins while spying down through surveillance cameras mounted on the hull. After several minutes in viewing the city wreckage his expression alighted with a broad grin when seeing people wandering near its base. Though unable to clearly identify his friends, the mere presence of survivors left him bursting with hope.

***

"I want to bury him," Sage said, quietly. "I don't want him to end up like the others." Brushing away his tears, he studied his blood-stained hands until seeing Heroin cover them with hers.

"I will carry his body away from the ruins," Adrenaline offered. "I cannot fathom where we should bury him. The cannibals may catch the scent of his body when decay begins, should they discover him before the cockroaches. Sage, I understand your wish for his body to not be desecrated by the monsters roaming out there. But, if I may, I would suggest we leave him here, entomb him in this place so his fate may be more humane."

"Yeah, we should leave him here. I just…wish we could take him back up to the sky. Bob wanted to see the moon again. But, none of us will now." Feeling Heroin wrap her arm around his shoulder, Sage rested his face against hers as she held him close. The trembling of his hands, and aching in his stomach, reminded Sage of when he found out his mom was gone. This also recalled his memory of when his mom told him his dad was gone. Sage felt unsure of how many more times he could endure people he loved disappearing from his life. But he knew this horrific place was not through with torturing him.

Picking up and holding Bob's dead body in his arms, Adrenaline looked to the others before carrying him into the storage room. Returning minutes later, he closed the door behind him and both he and Lithium began barricading the storage room entrance in hopes of sealing Bob's final resting place from the cannibals.

"I should help," Sage mumbled, under his breath.

"No," Heroin responded, refusing to let go of his hands. "They are capable of managing this task on their own. Please rest here. My heart breaks in watching how you suffer his loss and grieve for others who have vanished from your life. And I beg you not to mourn my passing, for I am still here and intend to remain by your side. This I promise."

"I wish you were safe, all of you, but I'm glad you're here with me," Sage mumbled. Heroin caressed his cheek in response to this.

"We should go," Adrenaline urged, once finished. "We may find refuge in another part of the city ruins, one offering better defense and a way for escape if needed."

"Should we wait until the storm passes?" Heroin asked.

"The storm will never pass," Sage responded, vacantly. "It will always be there."

"I'm falling in love with you," he confessed, sensing her lips pressing against his cheek, and reeling from sadness and grew anxious in watching for her response.

"A confession I have yearned for as I have *already* fallen for you," she answered, her smile corrupted by tears. Sharing a tender kiss, he brushed strands of her hair away from her face and rested his forehead against hers.

"Come on," Sage urged, helping Heroin to her feet. Leading them through the science lab, after struggling down the bent metal staircase, Sage continued to the main doorway and stepped through before helping Heroin out. But after doing so, both stood paralyzed in watching the last traces of a *messiah shaft* disappear in the sky. A part of Sage felt happy in witnessing this shaft of light, leaving him wondering if God had called Bob's eternal soul home.

Something, though, appeared off as he continued staring forward. An unmoving light hovering in the sky drew and held firm his attention.

"That cannot be what I believe it is," he heard Lithium utter.

Further revealed by violent strikes of lightning, Sage's breath rushed from his lungs when spotting the silhouette of a skyjammer.

"How?" he whispered. Yet his question went unanswered when hearing a startled scream from Heroin. Noticing her shielding herself behind him, Sage turned his head and then stumbled back in realizing they weren't alone.

***

Adjusting the clarity of the camera lens, in seeking better focus, expelling all air from his lungs, William watched in horror as the people he spied through the surveillance camera chased down a man, dragging him to the ground and then ripping off his clothes. Their actions turned heinous and vile, forcing him to clench his eyes shut. Stunned by such brutality, tremors of fear quaked through his body. Believing the man would not survive this horrific attack, William altered the camera's angle with the search for his friends now evermore desperate. Resolving this would not be their fate, he intensified his search.

Seeing another band of men climbing through the ruins, he noticed one waving his arms as if instructing the others to spread out. Clearly, they were engaged in tracking something, no, someone. There were no animals left to hunt, only people. To William, the sense of irony over this grew evident. Men once hunted animals. Now men behaved as animals in the hunting of other men.

Maneuvering the camera angle away from the hunting party, at first William found nothing in sight they could be tracking. But then, through the doorway of a severely damaged structure, Sage miraculously appeared followed by Heroin. His heart nearly exploded through his chest when seeing Adrenaline and Lithium step in view. All were safe. Yet, they *weren't*. Dread overtook elation in realizing the peril his friends unknowingly faced. They stood as unwitting prey, with the hunters drawing closer and closer.

***

Several men stood in front of them, their filthy clothing hanging in tatters on their skeletal-thin frames. Sage recognized the tallest instantly, being the one who'd killed Harley. Sniffing about like an animal, the continuous flashes of lightning revealed his wicked grin. Backing a step, Sage halted when the other men aggressively growled at him until the tall man raised his hand in silencing them.

"*We want her*," he rasped, harshly.

"No," Sage responded.

"*We...want...her*," the man repeated.

Crowding next to Sage and Heroin, Adrenaline and Lithium ignited intense growling and bellowing howls from the cannibals until once more stifled when the man again raised his hand.

"*I'm not asking,*" the man snarled. "*We are taking her.*"

"No," Sage refused, then grabbing a piece of rubble in threatening the man.

"*We will take her and then feast on your flesh.*"

"Why do you wait, *dog*?" Adrenaline taunted, in anger. The man burst to laughter when hearing this, his eyes brimming with insanity. "Not one of you will sink your fangs into our flesh. Come on with you. Be an obedient *bitch* and fetch this stick." From behind his back, Adrenaline revealed a metal rod which he launched like a javelin at the man. Piercing him through his chest, the man froze in place, his expression blank as he stood still for a moment before falling to his knees. A smile crept across his face with blood seeping from his mouth.

"*Thank you,*" he mumbled, and fell face forward further impaling the rod through his body.

Charging toward them, the others halted when blinded by rapid flashes of light and startled by a deafening roar. At first cowering, they stumbled away, soon disappearing from sight.

Holding steady to each other, when the lights dimmed, Sage noticed a lowered rope ladder flailing about. Overwhelmed by relief and excitement, he stumbled over ruble before grasping the bottom rung.

"Climb up! Hurry!" Sage urged.

Lithium climbed first, followed by Heroin and Adrenaline. When Sage reached the top of the ladder, firm hands helped pulled him up through the bottom hatch. Heaving for breath, his smile beamed at Lord Amphetamine, once more his rescuer.

Chapter Seventeen

"How?" Sage asked, in disbelief.

"Marisol," Lord Amphetamine replied, prompting Sage to nod in understanding. "We must make haste with our departure. I fear for our safety, as well as that of Marisol's. Follow me!"

Leading Sage up to the helm, Sage's surprise was evident as he looked on in awe at the fully repaired and improved control panels.

"All has been restored and modified," Lord Amphetamine confirmed. "She is now capable of both day and night travel, with ease, so I relinquish the helm of this magnificent vessel to its rightful pilot. I request thee to return us to the heavens, both dark and brilliant." Beaming his smile, Sage nodded again.

Collecting his bearings regarding the advanced controls, Sage then hurried in preparing the skyjammer's ascent through the storm clouds. Impressed by the confidence and ease Sage exuded behind the helm, Lord Amphetamine watch on in fascination. This was where his friend belonged, not as a prisoner or living artifact of a lost generation, but rather a pioneer bound to an expansive sun-lit frontier. There is where his fate would rest.

"Hang on. I'm going to initiate the thrusters," Sage confirmed, and then eased the helm and a lever to its side forward. Holding on, the two watched as blinding flashes of lightning appeared before them, as if taunting a challenge to their departure.

Feeling the skyjammer tremoring under their feet, Lord Amphetamine held his breath when they surged ahead toward the relentless lightning. Sensing gravity pulling at his back, he watched Sage fully engage the thrusters with the glowing and billowing, smoke-like storm drawing closer. Echoing blasts of thunder rung in their ears causing both to wince from their intensity. Violent, gusting winds assaulting the skyjammer nearly knocked it from its trajectory into the storm, yet Sage firmly grasped the helm, appearing to hold his breath while straining to hang on. Seeing the cloud cover so very close, his eyes clenched closed when blinded by a glaring explosion of lightning. With air rushing from his lungs, and his muscles flexing to hold tight from the gravitational pull, William silently offered a prayer to a God he felt uncertain still existed as they pierced the storm.

Tossed side-to-side, he collided with Sage, gripping the helm to assist him. Though battered by the storm's ferocity, the skyjammer maintained its speed. And not once did he doubt Sage's ability to pilot them through the tempest. Watching him, he could only feel awed by Sage's mastery as a pilot, exuding confidence in his natural ability and commanding admiration for his skills.

Breaching the storm clouds, once released by the strong gravitational pull both could breathe again. Their robust laughter erupted while embracing each other.

"*Brilliant*! Absolutely brilliant!" Lord Amphetamine exclaimed.

Looking toward the night sky, the moon cast its luminous glow over the endless expanse of clouds while commanding sole presence of the dark sky to their left. Stars too numerous to count were strewn across heaven in the opposite direction.

"Is that a star?" Sage wondered aloud, noticing a large distant flickering light.

"No, my friend. There…orbits the white city."

Understanding Sage's frightened reaction when taking a step back he attempted to ease his fear.

"No harm will come to you my friend," he vowed. "Yet...*I*...must return to the white city, and to Marisol. I have fallen deeply in love with her. I have *always* loved her. Please, I ask that you return me to her and then take leave of the white city. My friends must also remain with you. They were happiest in the sun. I wish only for that life for them."

"But what about Valorian?"

"The false god's reign has fallen, my friend. Onto a brave new world you will leave me."

"Are you sure?"

"Yes, my friend. Trust me."

"I do," Sage whispered, nodding his head. "Alright, I'll set a course for New London."

"Thank you," Lord Amphetamine responded, and embraced Sage.

Leaving Sage alone, he returned to the skyjammer's main living area. Seeing the others, before he could say anything, Heroin thrust herself into his arms.

"My lord, I held fear for your safety," she gushed, while embracing him.

"My dear, Evangeline, I am but a roguish cat having many lives ahead of me."

"Why do you refer to me by my true name?" Heroin asked, stunned by his response.

"Henceforth, I renounce the titles bestowed to each of you. Evermore, in my eyes, you shall be my dearest Evangeline, my esteemed Richard and my champion Brendan. No longer shall you be burdened by the scarlet titles of your afflictions."

"And what of you?" Evangeline wondered.

"I relinquish my title of Lord Amphetamine and reclaim my true identity, William." Glancing at Brendan and Richard, when noticing Richard struggle to stand and then ease down on the floor, William fretted. "What brings you to your knees, my friend?"

"He is ill," Brendan responded, on behalf of his friend. "He must return to the sunlight."

"Then a return to the sun, you shall have," William vowed. "Your new pilot will see to this. I hold deep regret, though, that I will not journey there with you." All appeared startled by this confession. "Please, hold no fear for me," he urged. "Valorian has fallen, his treachery is no more. I willingly return to the white city and to the woman who holds possession of my heart. There I will forge a new life with her...and will forever keep fond memories of you, my friends, well in my thoughts."

"My lord." Richard offered, extending his tremoring hand while clearly fighting back his sadness. Holding his friend's hand, Brendan and Evangeline joined their hands to theirs, echoing Richard's words.

"My friends." William smiled and responded, a tear streaming down his cheek.

***

Briefly closing her eyes from the fatigue she suffered, Marisol sat down on a stool next to the large table in her laboratory. Glancing at the daylighter artifacts, each piece held new meaning for her, exuding auras of cruelty and tragedy. Never more a valued collection of salvaged possession, the objects now represented the final remembrances of a race of human rendered extinct by a maniacal assassin hell-bent on claiming his twisted status as a god among men.

Confronted by a lack of desire to further examine and catalogue the artifacts, Marisol stood up and wandered over to the open laboratory door. Turning off the light, she closed the door behind her and walked away, uncertain if she would return the next day. Having received no word from William of his rescue attempt, very little in her life held meaning. And with New London and its citizenry evolving and unrecognizable, Marisol wondered where her place in this new society would be and felt uncertain this altering world would have meaning and purpose were she to exist alone amidst it.

While slowly strolling to her dormitory, evidence of bold and brash contempt regarding former conformity and behavior displayed among the citizenry. Euphoria and laughter were abundant, as were amorous demonstrations of affection. Love and passion, once deemed forbidden, had found prominence. In the central park, she noticed men holding hands with women while expressing their love for each other. Children at play foretold how the future generation would embrace these changes. And, though stunned when seeing two middle-aged men unabashedly engage in a passionate kiss, she found herself smiling in admiration of them. Yet, in being surrounded by such liveliness, none of what she witnessed could penetrate deep into the aching hollowness inside her. Minute-by minute, her spirit withered with loneliness.

Arriving at her dormitory, Marisol entered her small room without turning on a single light. What was there to see? The single bed and bureau, the kitchenette, the sterile white-tiled bathroom, nothing changed whether in the dark or by light. Even her reflection in the mirror would remain the same were she to turn on a lamp.

Yet when sitting on the edge of her bed, she felt something that had not been there before. Reaching for the lamp on her bureau, after turning it on, she jumped off the bed in shock of what had been left there for her. Touching, and then running her fingers over the fabric of an exquisite all black dress, never before had she seen a creation such as this. Paired with the dress were a brimmed hat and heeled boots of matching color as well as cosmetics, considered contraband before Valorian's fall.

Though distressed in wondering who could have left all this here, the overwhelming desire to try everything on would not be denied. With her heart and pulse racing,

Marisol stripped off her plain, Victorian-era skirt and blouse, and dressed in the outfit left for her. Stepping in front of her floor-length mirror, her jaw dropped while falling spellbound to her own reflection. Fetching the cosmetics off the bed, she completed her transformation with ruby-red lips and dazzling color applied to her eyelids.

Again studying her reflection, Marisol jumped when hearing a knock at her door. Glancing with dread, she trembled when seeing a note forced under her door. At first hesitant to retrieve it, taking a deep breath, Marisol picked it up and felt butterflies surging in her stomach as she read the hand-written words.

My lovely,

I obtained these gifts from the Black Alley, a forbidden shadowed section of the white city once frequented by members of the elite, a discrete setting for the satisfaction of their vices amidst pubs, opium dens, and even brothels. It has now become a popular destination as a red light district for the free. What do you say? Care to stroll with me to the dark side, my lovely? Be forewarned. I am standing outside your door in anticipation of your beauty.

William

Clutching the note to her heaving chest, Marisol stepped over to her door, pressing her ear against the cold surface. Hearing nothing, she grasped the handle and slowly lured it down until it unlatched. And once opening it, William's devilish smile ignited a fire within her soul, finally understanding Sage's desire to feel burned. The scorching sensation radiating deep inside her proved indescribable from anything she had ever felt before, leading her to wonder if she was experiencing true life for the first time.

"Going' my way, lovely?" William asked.

Smiling, Marisol extended her hand to him and watched as he adorned it with a soft kiss.

***

Eight months later

Hearing Evangeline walk up behind him, Sage smiled when feeling her fingers gently caress and roam up his back. Easing in front of him at the helm, Sage wrapped his arms around her as she rested her head against his bare chest. Taking hold of one of his hands, she pressed it to her stomach, allowing him to feel the sensation of their unborn child's subtle movements. Sage smiled when noticing a kick.

"Are you happy here?" he asked, kissing Evangeline on her head.

"*Never* have I been so happy," she replied, nestling her head deeper against him.

"I love you," he whispered in her ear, causing her to look up so they could share a kiss.

Again resting her head against him, for a while they stood there, gazing out at the sunny vista ahead of them. Though they'd found no traces of other daylighters who'd escaped Valorian's genocide, Sage hoped that somewhere out there daylighters still existed. To himself, he resolved to never stop trying to find them.

This tranquil moment spent with Evangeline ended when Brendan appeared.

"I have come to relieve you at the helm. Go on with you both. Just try to keep the noise down after you two crawl in bed…or whatever your intentions are. Richard just fell asleep."

"How is he today?" Sage asked, always concerned for him.

"His spirit is resilient as always, yet his migraines and fatigue persist," Brendan confirmed. "It was my hope…he would show signs of improvement by now, however—."

Touching Brendan's shoulder, Sage tried coaxing a smile from him, finding success in luring only a slight grin.

"Have faith."

"Always," Brendan responded. "I simply wish I could best him in chess just *once*." He smiled.

As Sage and Evangeline were leaving, Brendan stopped them.

"Hold on. We received a communication from the colonists in New Zealand. They appear to be thriving considerably, calling their settlement *Middle Earth*, though I fail to understand their foolish meaning of this, a confusing reference regarding a *lord* and jewelry, *rings* I believe. They are a rather spirited bunch. Anyway, their invitation for us to join with them stands. We will always be welcome there."

"Do you wish to join them?" Sage asked, feelingly slightly anxious for his response.

"No," Brendan responded, quickly. "Like you, my friend, the sunlight is where I wish to be. I speak for Richard, as well. All of you are my family. I believe this is where we *all* wish to dwell."

Feeling relieved, Sage beamed.

"Good. Good night, big brother," Sage offered, finally getting Brendan to smile. At first, following Evangeline down to the living quarters, Sage stopped for a moment to stare out through the windows at the distant sun-lit horizon behind them, always careful in watching for any traces of the edge of night.

The End

About Jeffery Martin Botzenhart

I've been waiting for you to finish this book. I hope you enjoyed the story. So what do you think of it? I know. You're at a loss of words over it's brilliance, or something like that. So now you want to know about me. I don't really like talking about myself, but I'll indulge you the answer to a few questions. Favorite color? Blue. Favorite food? Pizza and Oreos (not Oreo's on pizza, that's gross). Favorite Movie? Tron. Am I an illegal alien? Only when abducted by Martians (being taken against my will is illegal). Check out my social media links to learn more about the genius me who wrote this incredible book.

Social Media

Facebook:
www.facebook.com/jefferymartinbotzenhartwritingjourney

Twitter: https://twitter.com/JBotzenhart@JBotzenhart

If you enjoyed this story, check out these other Solstice Publishing books by Jeffery Martin Botzenhart:

Daybreak

Amidst a world of cyber surveillance and advancing technology of 2035 San Francisco, Sebastian, a teen runaway, innocently access a sophisticated virtual reality program. The breach of this data proves the catalyst in unraveling corporate and government sanctioned deception of the most unimaginable type. And along with his computer hacker friend, Scotty, both are thrust into a dangerous conspiracy, linking them to a source exposing the truth.

https://www.amazon.com/dp/B073SB9BXG

After Dark

With Sebastian's health deteriorating, his dad decides to risk them both crossing into Canada in efforts to meet with a physician friend in Montreal who might be able to help. Yet before even reaching the border they encounter new threats against them. Their escape is further complicated when after reaching Lee's friend they are separated. This leads Sebastian to a perilous journey across the Canadian frontier, finding both a new friend and discovering a far more dangerous robotic conspiracy than anyone could have imagined.

https://www.amazon.com/dp/B0778SL11P

Dead of Night

Sebastian's hopes of having a new life in Alaska quickly fade. Suffering in being the constant target for teasing from his high school classmates and understanding the dangers his dad attempts to shield them from, a sudden tragedy destroys any chances of this. He returns to San Francisco with the belief he can resume his previous life there as a runaway surviving on the streets. But as the old saying warns, you can't go home. The dangers he faces here have multiplied, leading him to wonder if he can ever escape from the relentless hauntings of his past.

https://www.amazon.com/dp/B078SCFX77

First Light

Emotionally suffering from what has happened to them, both Sebastian and Ben set out separately to confront their demons. Little do they realize how and when their paths will soon cross. For Sebastian, seeking closure in what happened to his dad and sister is what he most needs. For Ben, his growing rage consumes his desire for revenge.

https://www.amazon.com/dp/B079LK7TML

Harvest Fever

Bullied by classmates and abused by his stepdad, seventeen year old Orrville Fletcher plans to leave his run-down home outside Birchwood Hollow, Tennessee once he turns eighteen. But one night after fighting off his stepdad, his escape from this small remote town in Appalachia is halted by an unimaginable invasion of space aliens, leading him to revelations of an unexpected truth.

https://www.amazon.com/dp/B074JZV44F

www.ingramcontent.com/pod-product-compliance
Lightning Source LLC
Chambersburg PA
CBHW070911030726
47504CB00005B/1559